The Gothic Tales
of the
Marquis de Sade

The Gothic Tales
of the
Marquis de Sade

*Translated from the French and with
an Introduction by
Margaret Crosland*

Peter Owen
London and Chester Springs

PETER OWEN PUBLISHERS
73 Kenway Road, London SW5 0RE

Peter Owen books are distributed in the USA by
Dufour Editions Inc., Chester Springs, PA 19425-0007

Translated from the French
Contes et Fabliaux d'un Troubadour Provençal du XVIIIe Siècle

First published in Great Britain in 1965 as
Eugénie de Franval and Other Stories
by Neville Spearman Ltd
First published by Peter Owen 1990
This paperback edition published 2005
© Margaret Crosland 1965, 1990

ISBN 0 7206 1251 9

A catalogue record for this book is available from the British Library.

Printed and bound in Great Britain by Bookmarque Ltd, Croydon, Surrey

CONTENTS

INTRODUCTION

Over the centuries the titles of some books have become household words, but only a very few authors have given their names to nouns, adjectives and adverbs in several languages, terms for which there is no simple equivalent or alternative. The Marquis de Sade, who lived from 1740 to 1814 was one such writer. He became Comte on the death of his father in 1767 but has always been known in his native France and beyond by his earlier title. His major works were written, and some of them published, between the 1780s and 1800 while many others, including his letters, did not reach the public until after his death, in some cases having been discovered only in the twentieth century. The group of words to which he gave his name has needed explanations which go beyond etymology. 'Infamous for his crimes and the character of his writings', says the *Shorter Oxford Dictionary* (1973), adding that the word 'sadism' was first used in 1888 and means 'a form of sexual perversion marked by a love of cruelty'. *Chambers 20th Century Dictionary* (1983) records that Sade died insane, a fact disputed by scholars and biographers, even if, after many years in prison, he spent his last eleven years in the madhouse of Charenton, a few miles outside Paris.

During the nineteenth century Sade, if read, or indeed if known at all, was regarded as no more than a sexual pervert, unmentionable in civilized society, a writer of obscenities which exceeded even those fashionable in his day. His work was useful to a few unscrupulous publishers and booksellers who were delighted to make money by selling his 'forbidden' books in secret. When, in the early twentieth century, the poet Guillaume Apollinaire also tried to earn money by writing erotic novels,* he studied Sade and wrote about him, rescuing him from a shadowy life as a mere pornographer. Apollinaire has remained one of his most perceptive interpreters. As he looked beyond the catalogues of perversions and crimes in Sade's most outspoken books the poet realized that here was one of the most misunderstood writers of the eighteenth century, condemned by critics who had failed to see him in a social, psychological and political context. Later, in Britain, Aldous Huxley noted that the works of the Marquis contained 'more philosophy than pornography'. Readers who first come to Sade in search of sexual excitement soon realize that he was not writing only for that purpose. He did not compose lengthy descriptions of unthinkable cruelties merely to titillate or corrupt his readers: he was anxious to attract their attention because he wanted to communicate, with a kind of desperate intensity, all that he felt about human behaviour, about morality, about individual and social problems. He wanted to write about the unlimited potential of human beings, but he was writing long before anyone had established a scientific system for doing so. He was often limited to using physiology, not psychology, as his starting point, for he knew no other way of analysing behaviour or expressing his findings.

Sade's range was much wider than is usually thought. In addition to his major works, *Justine, Juliette, La Philosophie dans le Boudoir, Les 120 Journées de Sodome*, to name his most famous or infamous titles, he wrote historical novels, plays, an anti-Bonaparte satire, *Zoloé* (although some dispute his authorship), and the vast fiction *Aline et Valcour*, a *roman à tiroirs* which includes shorter novels within the main novel. For the late twentieth-century reader his most accessible fiction can be found in the stories entitled *Les Crimes de l'Amour* (1800 and later),

*e.g., *Les Onze Mille Verges* (Peter Owen, 1976)

which were prefaced by an essay on the novel. Some of these stories were published during Sade's lifetime, some as late as 1927. There were fifty in all, the full title of the collection being *Historiettes, contes et fabliaux d'un troubadour du XVIIIe siècle*. Some are comic anecdotes, some are examples of eighteenth century *galanterie* and occasionally illustrate Sade's taste for irony. The longer ones, like *Eugénie de Franval* and *Florville et Courval*, are best described as Gothic, written possibly under the influence of English writers such as Horace Walpole, whose *The Castle of Otranto* was translated in 1767.

The 'Gothic' stories have a quality of suspense, for the reader does not know what will happen to the incestuous Franval and his daughter. It is equally hard to guess why Florville does not want to marry Courval – and who was the unknown murderess in the *auberge* at Nancy? If Franval's defence of incest seems to be related in tone to some of the more outrageous speeches in *La Philosophie dans le Boudoir*, vice is punished and, in the end, virtue triumphs.

In many of Sade's serious tales women, such as the wretched Justine, are the principal victims. If they attempt to take control of their own lives they are usually defeated by men. Sade himself treated most women badly, but unexpectedly this forward-looking writer had some notion of their potential. In *Aline et Valcour* he described an ideal country, Tamoé, where women would enjoy equality with men; this was part of his grandiose plan for individual liberty. If, thought Sade, so many women were forced into a life of deceit and treachery before they could earn any minor personal success, whose fault was that? In the story *Le Cocu de lui-même* (*The Self-Made Cuckold*), the author attempted to explain: men treated women so badly that they had only themselves to blame for the behaviour of their wives and mistresses.

Apollinaire suggested that Sade chose heroines rather than heroes for his two major novels because he considered women to be superior to men. Nearly two centuries after his death Sade continues to produce surprises, even for the feminists. The leading French feminist of the twentieth century, Simone de Beauvoir, wrote her challenging study *Must We Burn de Sade?* in 1952 and three years later it was published with two other essays in a volume aptly entitled *Privilèges*. In eighteenth-century France few people enjoyed greater privileges than Sade, for as a member of an old-established aristocratic family he was free to behave more or less as he wished; but when he eloped with his wife's sister he had forgotten one thing: his wife's mother, the Marquise de Montreuil, was just as privileged as he was, and richer. If Sade spent so much time in prison or on the run it was not so much because he was a law-breaker, it was because he had infuriated a middle-aged woman. If he had not behaved so unconventionally, even in eighteenth-century terms, the Marquise could not have forced his imprisonment without trial under the autocratic system of the *lettre de cachet*. And the imprisoned Marquis would probably not have written all he did in the way he did.

The Gothic framework which Sade used in his longer stories, and the horseplay he included in his anecdotal fiction, allowed him to entertain his contemporaries and half-concealed his main purpose: he was a moralist. In 1909 Apollinaire prophesied that Sade might well dominate the twentieth century and in some ways he was proved right: scientific and technological progress has not been matched by any reduction in cruel, 'sadistic' behaviour on an individual or national scale. Incest and child abuse may even be on the increase, marriages crumble, women still have no equality with men. Sade anticipated the extremes of human behaviour which are now exposed, but rarely mitigated, every day throughout the world. He made a concentrated effort to describe them. He even attempted, remembering his own problems, to give latter-day readers some advice, usually ironic, on the perennial problems of marital behaviour. Simone de Beauvoir was surely right when she said of Sade in 1952, 'The supreme value of his testimony is that it disturbs us.'

M.C.

EUGENIE DE FRANVAL
A Tragic Story

OUR ONLY MOTIVE in writing this story is the instruction of mankind and the betterment of their way of life. May all readers become fully aware of the great peril that always dogs those who do as they wish in order to satisfy their desires. May they be convinced that good upbringing, riches, talents and the gifts bestowed by nature are only likely to lead people astray when restraint, good conduct, wisdom and modesty are not there to support them or turn them to good account: these are the truths that we are going to put into action. May we be forgiven the unnatural details of the horrible crime of which we are forced to speak; is it possible to make such deviations detestable if one has not the courage to present them openly?

Rarely does everything harmonise in the same being to lead him to prosperity; if he is favoured by nature then fortune refuses him her gifts; if fortune is liberal with her favours then nature treats him badly; it appears that the hand of Heaven wishes to show us that in each individual, as in its most sublime operations, the laws of equilibrium are the first laws of the Universe, the ones which simultaneously regulate everything that happens, everything that vegetates and everything that breathes.

Franval, who lived in Paris, where he was born, possessed, along with an income of 400,000 livres, the finest figure, the most pleasant face and the most varied talents; but beneath this attractive exterior lay hidden every vice, and unfortunately those of which the adoption and habitual indulgence lead so rapidly to crime. An imagination more unbridled than anything one can depict was Franval's prime defect; men of this type do not mend their ways, the decline of power makes them worse; the less they can do, the more they undertake; the less they achieve, the more they invent; each age brings new ideas, and satiety, far from cooling their ardour, only prepares the way for more fatal refinements.

As we said, Franval possessed in profusion all the amenities of youth, all the talents which enhance it; but since he was full of disdain for moral and religious duties it had become impossible for his tutors to make him adopt any of them.

In a century when the most dangerous books are in the hands of children, as in those of their fathers and teachers, when the temerity of obstinacy passes for philosophy, unbelief for strength and licentiousness for imagination, the young Franval's wit was greeted with laughter, a moment later perhaps he was scolded for it, then he was praised. Franval's father, a great supporter of the fashionable sophistries, was the first to encourage his son to think seriously about all these matters; he himself lent him all the works which could corrupt him more rapidly; what teacher would have dared, after that, to inculcate principles different from those of the household where he was obliged to please?

In any case, Franval lost his parents when he was still very young, and at the age of nineteen, an old uncle, who himself died shortly afterwards, assigned him, while arranging his marriage, all the possessions that were to belong to him one day.

Monsieur de Franval, with such a fortune, should easily have found a wife; an infinite number of candidates presented themselves, but since he had begged his uncle to give him only a girl younger than himself, and with as few people around her as possible, the old relative, in order to satisfy his nephew, let his choice fall upon a certain Mademoiselle de Farneille, the daughter of a financier, possessing now only a mother, still young in fact, but with 60,000 livres of very real income; the girl was fifteen, and had the most delightful physiognomy to be found in Paris at that time . . . one of those virginal faces, in which innocence and charm are depicted together, in the delicate features of love and the graces . . . fine blonde hair floating below her waist, large blue eyes expressing tenderness and modesty, a slender, supple and slight figure, with a lily-white skin and the freshness of roses, full of talents, a very lively imagination, but with a touch of sadness, a little of that gentle melancholy which leads to a love of books and solitude; attributes which nature seems to grant only to the individuals whom her hand destines to misfortunes, as though to make them less bitter, through that sober and touching voluptuousness that they enjoy in feeling them, and which makes them prefer tears to the frivolous joy of happiness, much less effective and much less penetrating.

Madame de Farneille, who was thirty-two when her daughter was married, was also witty and attractive, but perhaps slightly too reserved and severe; since she desired the happiness of her only child, she had consulted the whole of Paris about this match; and since she no longer had any relatives and her only advisers were some of those cold friends to whom everything is indifferent, people convinced her that the young man who was being offered to her daughter was without any doubt the best she could find in Paris, and that she would commit an unforgivable folly if she failed to agree to this match, it therefore took place: and the young people, who were rich enough to take their own house, settled in it at once.

In young Franval's heart were none of those vices of frivolity, restlessness or foolishness which prevent a man from being fully developed before thirty; understanding himself very well, liking order, perfectly capable of running a house, Franval possessed all the necessary qualities for this aspect of the enjoyment of life. His vices, of a totally different kind, were indeed rather the faults of maturity than the inconsistencies of youth . . . artfulness, intrigue, . . . malice, baseness, selfishness, much diplomacy and trickery, while all this was concealed not only by the graces and talents already mentioned but even by eloquence and infinite wit and by the most seductive external appearance. Such was the man whom we have to depict.

Mademoiselle de Farneille, who, in accordance with custom, had known her husband for a month at the most before allying herself to him, deceived by this false brilliance, had been taken in by him; the days were not long enough for the pleasure of contemplating him, she idolised him, and things had even reached the point when people would have feared for this young person if any obstacle had upset the delights of a marriage in which she found, she said, the only happiness of her life.

As for Franval, who was philosophical about women as about all other things in life, he had considered this delightful person with utter coolness.

'The wife who belongs to us,' he would say, 'is a kind of individual whom custom has made subservient to us; she must be gentle, submissive . . . very demure, not that I am concerned with the prejudices of dishonour which a wife can bring upon us when she imitates our licentiousness; but one does not like the idea that someone else is contemplating the removal of our rights; all the rest is immaterial and adds nothing to happiness.'

When a husband feels this way it is easy to prophesy that there are no roses in store for the unfortunate girl who is allied to him. Madame de Franval, who was honourable, sensitive, well brought up and anticipated through love the wishes of the only man in the world who occupied her, wore her chains for the first few years without suspecting her enslavement; it was easy for her to see that she was only gleaning the fields of marriage, but she was still too happy with what was left to her and her only care, her closest attention was directed to the fact that during those brief moments granted to her affection, Franval could at least encounter all that she believed to be necessary to the happiness of this beloved husband.

The best proof of all, however, which Franval still did not exclude from his duties, was that during the first year of his marriage his wife, then aged sixteen and a half, gave birth to a daughter even more beautiful than her mother, and whom the father at once named Eugénie . . . Eugénie, both the horror and the miracle of nature.

Monsieur de Franval, who, as soon as this child was born, no doubt formed the most detestable designs on her, immediately separated her from her mother. Until the age of seven, Eugénie was entrusted to women of whom Franval was sure and who, limiting their endeavours to forming a good constitution and teaching her to read, took care not to give her any knowledge of religious or moral principles, about which a girl of her age should normally be instructed.

Madame de Farneille and her daughter, who were very shocked by this conduct, reproached Monsieur de Franval about it; he replied phlegmatically that since his plan was to make his daughter happy, he did not want to force upon her fantasies which were only likely to frighten people without ever becoming useful to them; that a girl whose only need was to learn how to please could at best be unaware of this nonsense, of which the imaginary existence, in disturbing the calm of her life, would give her no additional moral truth and no additional physical grace. Such remarks caused immediate displeasure to Madame de Farneille who, as she moved away from the pleasures of this world, was going closer to thoughts of heaven. Piety is a weakness dependent on age or health. When the passions are at their height a future which one believes to be very distant usually causes little uneasiness, but when their language is less lively, as we near the end . . . when finally everything leaves us, we cast ourselves again into the bosom of the God whom we heave heard mentioned in childhood, and if according to the philosophers these later illusions are as fantastic as the others, they are at least not so dangerous.

Since Franval's mother-in-law had no longer any relatives, little credit on her own, and at the most, as we have said, a few of those casual friends . . . who avoid responsibility if we put them to the test, having to struggle against a likeable, young and well-placed son-in-law, imagined very sensibly that it was simpler to keep to representations rather than to undertake stringent measures, with a man who would ruin the mother and have the daughter locked up, if they dared to stand up to him; in the meantime Madame de Farneille merely hazarded a few remonstrances and became silent as soon as she saw that this was achieving nothing.

Franval, sure of his superiority, seeing clearly that he was feared, soon renounced all scruples concerning anything whatsoever, and contenting himself with some slight concealment, simply because of the public, went straight to his horrible goal.

As soon as Eugénie reached the age of seven, Franval took her to his wife; and this loving mother, who had not seen her child since she had brought her into the world, unable to have her fill of caresses, held her for two hours pressed against her bosom, covering her with kisses, bathing her with tears. She wanted to know what talents she possessed, but Eugénie had none beyond reading fluently, enjoying the most robust health and of being angelically beautiful. Madame de Franval was again in despair when she realised that it was only too true that her daughter was unaware of even the first principles of religion.

'What is this, sir,' she said to her husband, 'are you therefore bringing her up only for this world? Will you not deign to reflect that she will only inhabit it for a moment like us, and afterwards will plunge into eternity, which will certainly be fatal if you deprive her of what can make her enjoy there a happy fate at the feet of the Being from whom she received life.'

'If Eugénie knows nothing, madame,' replied Franval, 'if these maxims are carefully concealed from her, she could not be unhappy; for if they are true, the Supreme Being is too fair to punish her for her ignorance, and if they are false, why mention them to her? As regards the other needs of her education, have confidence in me, I beg you; from today I am to be her teacher, and I assure you that in a few years' time your daughter will surpass all children of her age.'

Madame de Franval tried to insist, invoking the eloquence of the heart to assist that of reason, shedding some tears; but Franval, who was unmoved by them, did not even seem to notice them; he had Eugénie taken away, saying to his wife that if she considered opposing in any way the education which he hoped to give his daughter, or if she suggested to him principles different from those which he proposed to instil in her, she would deprive herself of the pleasure of seeing her, and that he would send his daughter to one of his châteaux from which she would never emerge again. Madame de Franval, who had become used to submission, was silent; she begged her husband not to separate her from such a treasured possession and promised, weeping, not to disturb in any way the education that was being prepared for her.

From this moment Mademoiselle de Franval was placed in a very fine apartment next to that of her father, with a highly intelligent governess, an undergoverness, a chambermaid and two little girls of her own age, who were there for the sole purpose of relaxation. She was given teachers for writing, drawing, poetry, natural history, declamation, geography, astronomy, anatomy, Greek, English, German, Italian, together with instructors for handling weapons, dancing, riding and music. Eugénie rose every day at seven o'clock, whatever the season she ran about the garden eating a large piece of rye bread, which formed her breakfast; she came in at eight o'clock, spent a few moments in her father's apartment, while he played with her or taught her little society games; until nine o'clock she prepared her work; then the first teacher arrived and she received five of them until two o'clock. She took her meal separately with her two friends and her chief governess. The dinner consisted of vegetables, fish, pastries and fruit, never any meat, soup, wine, liqueurs or coffee. From three o'clock to four, Eugénie went back into the garden to play for an hour with her little companions; they played together at tennis, ball-games, skittles, battledore and shuttlecock, or at running races; they wore comfortable clothing according to the season; nothing constricted their waists; they were never fastened into those ridiculous whalebones, which are equally dangerous for the stomach and the chest and which, hindering a young person's breathing, must necessarily harm the lungs. From four to six o'clock Mademoiselle de Franval received more teachers; and since they could not all appear in twenty-four hours, the remainder came during the next day. Three times a week Eugénie went to the theatre with her father, sitting in a little box with gratings, hired for her by the year. At nine o'clock she returned home and took supper, being served only with vegetables and fruit. From ten to eleven o'clock, four times a week, Eugénie played with her women, read a few novels and then went to bed. She spent the three other days, when Franval did not take supper away from home, alone in her father's apartment, and this time was employed in what Franval called his 'lectures'. During these he instilled into his daughter his maxims on morals and religion; on one side he showed her what some people thought about these matters and on the other he set out what he accepted himself.

Since she had much wit, wide knowledge, a lively intelligence and passions which were already aroused, it is easy to judge of the progress made by such ideas in Eugénie's mind; but since the object of the unworthy Franval was not only to strengthen the mind, his lectures rarely ended without stirring up the emotions; and this horrible man had found so skilfully the means of pleasing his daughter, he seduced her with such art, he made himself so useful in her instruction and her relaxation, he anticipated with such ardour everything which could please her, that Eugénie, in the midst of the most brilliant circles, found no one as attractive as her father; and even before the latter explained himself, the innocent and weak creature had accumulated in her young heart all the feelings of love, gratitude and affection which must necessarily lead to the most ardent desire; Franval was the only man in the world to her; she could distinguish only him, she was revolted by the idea of everything that could separate him from her; she would have given him not her honour, not her charms—for all these sacrifices would have seemed too slight for the moving object of her idolatry—but her blood, her very life, if this tender companion of her soul had demanded it.

This was not the case as far as Mademoiselle de Franval's feelings for her worthy and unfortunate mother were concerned. Her father skilfully told Eugénie that Madame de Franval, being his wife, demanded from him attention which often made him unable to do everything for his dear Eugénie that his feelings dictated; he had found the secret of instilling into this young person's heart much more hate and jealousy than the kind of respectable and affectionate feelings which should have arisen for such a mother.

'My friend, my brother,' Eugénie would sometimes say to Franval, who did not want his daughter to use any other expressions with him ... 'this woman whom you call your wife, this creature who, according to you, brought me into the world, must therefore be very demanding, since in wanting you always with her, she deprives me of the happiness of spending my life with you ... I see it clearly, you prefer her to your Eugénie. As far as I am concerned, I will never love anything which takes your heart away from me.'

'My dear friend,' replied Franval, 'no, nobody whatsoever in the entire world will acquire such powerful rights as yours; the ties which exist between this woman and your best friend are the result of custom and social conventions; I regard them in a philosophical light, and they will never affect those which bind us together ... you will always be the one preferred, Eugénie; you will be the angel and the light of my days, the focus of my soul and the purpose of my existence.'

'Oh, how sweet are these words!' replied Eugénie, 'repeat them often, my friend ... If you knew how pleasing to me are the expressions of your tenderness.'

She took Franval's hand and pressed it to her heart.

'Yes, yes, I feel them all here,' she went on.

'How your tender caresses assure me of that,' replied Franval, clasping her in his arms . . . And in this way, without any remorse, the traitor completed the seduction of the unfortunate girl.

However, Eugénie was reaching her fourteenth year, the moment when Franval wanted to consummate his crime. He did so. Let us shudder!

The very day when she reached this age, or rather that on which her fourteenth year was completed, they both found themselves in the country, with no relatives present and no one to disturb them. On that day the Count, having caused his daughter to be dressed like the virgins who in the past were consecrated in the temple of Venus, led her, at eleven o'clock in the morning, into a voluptuously decorated drawing-room where the daylight was softened by gauze curtains and the furniture strewn with flowers. In the centre stood a throne of roses; Franval led his daughter towards it.

'Eugénie,' he told her, seating her upon it, 'be today the queen of my heart, and let me adore you on my knees.'

'Let you adore me, my brother, when it is I who owe you everything, when you created me and brought me up! Ah, let me rather fall at your feet; this is the only place for me, and with you it is the only one to which I aspire.'

'Oh, my tender Eugénie,' said the Count, taking his place near her on the flower-strewn cushions which were to serve his triumph, 'if it is true that you owe me something, if in fact the feelings you have for me are as sincere as you say, do you know how to convince me of it?'

'How, my brother? Tell me quickly so that I can understand at once.'

'All these charms, Eugénie, that nature has so liberally bestowed upon you, all these attentions with which she has beautified you, must be sacrificed to me immediately.'

'But what are you asking me? Are you not master of

---

* The passages we give in italics, and which do not appear in the original edition, are those which Maurice Heine had found among de Sade's rough drafts (BN, manuscript 4010, editor's note).

everything? Does not your creation belong to you, can anyone else enjoy your handiwork?'

'But you realise the prejudices of men . . .'

'You have in no way concealed them from me.'

'I do not therefore want to go against them without your agreement.'

'Do you not despise them as I do?'

'That is so, but I do not want to tyrannise you, much less seduce you; I want to receive the favours I seek from love alone. You know what the world is like, I have hidden none of its attractions from you. To hide men from your sight, to let you see nobody except myself, would have been a deception unworthy of me; if there exists in the universe a being whom you prefer to me, name him at once, I will go to the ends of the earth to find him and will lead him to your arms at once. In fact it is your happiness that I want, my angel, your happiness much more than mine; the sweet pleasures that you can give me would be nothing to me if they were not the price of your love. Decide, therefore, Eugénie. The moment has come when you are to be sacrificed, you must be. But you yourself must name the man who will carry out the sacrifice, I renounce the pleasures that this title ensures for me if I do not receive them from your heart; and if it is not I whom you prefer, I shall always be worthy of your feelings in bringing you the one whom you can love. If I have not been able to captivate your heart, I will at least have deserved your affection; and I shall be Eugénie's friend, having failed to become her lover.'

'You shall be everything, brother, you shall be everything,' said Eugénie, burning with love and desire. 'To whom do you want me to sacrifice myself, if it is not to the only man whom I adore? What being in the universe can be more worthy than you of these poor charms that you desire . . . and which your burning hands are already caressing with ardour! Do you not see from the fire that consumes me that I am as anxious as you to experience the pleasure of which you tell me? Ah, take me, take me, my loving brother, my best friend, make Eugénie your victim; sacrificed by your beloved hands she will always be triumphant.'

The ardent Franval, who, in accordance with his character,

had only armed himself with so much delicacy in order to seduce with more finesse, soon took advantage of this daughter's credulity and, with all obstacles removed, as much through the principles with which he had nourished this soul that was open to all kinds of impressions, as through the art with which he captivated her at the last moment, he completed his perfidious conquest, and with impunity destroyed the virginity which by nature and by right it was his responsibility to defend.

Several days passed in mutual intoxication. Eugénie, who was old enough to know the pleasures of love, was encouraged by his methods and abandoned herself to it with enthusiasm. Franval taught her all love's mysteries and mapped out all its routes; the more he increased his adoration the better he enslaved his conquest. She would have like to receive him in a thousand temples at once, accusing him of not allowing his imagination to stray far enough; she thought he was concealing something from her. She complained of her age and of an ingenuousness which perhaps did not make her seductive enough: and if she wanted more instruction it was so that no means of arousing her lover could remain unknown to her.

They returned to Paris, but the criminal pleasures which had intoxicated this perverse man had given too much delectable enjoyment to his physical and moral faculties for the inconstancy which usually destroyed all his other intrigues to sever the ties of this one. He fell desperately in love, and this dangerous passion led inevitably to the most cruel abandonment of his wife . . . Alas, what a victim she was! Madame de Franval, then thirty-one years old, was at the height of her beauty; an air of sadness which was inevitable in view of the sorrows that consumed her, made her more intriguing still; bathed in tears, crushed by melancholy, her beautiful hair carelessly flowing loose over her alabaster bosom, her lips pressed amorously to the beloved portrait of her faithless tyrant, she resembled those beautiful virgins whom Michelangelo painted in the midst of sorrow: but she was still unaware of what was to complete her torment. The way in which Eugénie was being educated, the essential things of which she was left in ignorance, or which were only mentioned to her in order to make her hate them; her certainty that these duties, despised by Franval, would never be permitted to her daughter; the brief time she was allowed to see the girl, the fear that the unusual education she was receiving would sooner or later lead her to crime, the eccentricities of Franval in fact, his daily harshness towards her . . . she who was occupied only in anticipating his wishes, who knew no other charms except those which would interest or please him; until now these had been the only causes of her affliction. What sorrow was to pierce this loving and sensitive soul as soon as she learned everything!

However, Eugénie's education continued; she herself had wished to continue with her teachers until the age of sixteen, and her talents, her extensive knowledge, the graces which were developing in her each day, everything enslaved Franval more strongly; it was easy to see that he had never loved anyone as he loved Eugénie.

In Mademoiselle de Franval's external life nothing had been changed except the times of the lectures; these intimate discussions with her father became much more frequent and lasted long into the night. Only Eugénie's governess was informed of this intrigue and they trusted her enough not to fear any indiscretion on her part. There were also some changes in the arrangements for Eugénie's meals, she now took them with her parents. In a house such as Franval's this soon caused Eugénie to meet other people, and to be desired as a wife. Several people asked for her hand. Franval, who was certain of his daughter's heart, had not thought it at all necessary to fear these approaches, but he had not realised sufficiently that this rush of proposals might perhaps succeed in revealing everything.

During a conversation with her daughter, a favour so desired by Madame de Franval, and one she obtained so rarely, this affectionate mother informed Eugénie that Monsieur de Colunce wished to marry her.

'You know this man, my daughter,' said Madame de Franval; 'he loves you, he is young and likeable; he will be rich, he merely awaits your consent . . . your consent only, my daughter . . . how shall I reply?'

Eugénie, taken by surprise, blushed and replied that she felt no taste for marriage as yet, but that her father could be consulted; she would have no wishes other than his.

Madame de Franval saw this reply only as straight-forward, waited patiently for some days and, finding at last an opportunity to mention it to her husband, she communicated to him the intentions of the young Colunce's family and those that he had revealed himself, to which she added her daughter's reply.

It can well be imagined that Franval knew everything; but he nevertheless succeeded in disguising this without showing too much self-control.

'Madame,' he said drily to his wife, 'I ask you earnestly not to involve Eugénie in this; the care you have seen me take to remove her from you must have made it easy for you to recognise how much I wanted all that concerned her to have nothing to do with you. I renew my orders to you on this subject . . . you will not forget them, I imagine?'

'But how should I reply, sir, since it is I whom they ask?'

'You will say that I appreciate the honour they show me, and that my daughter has defects dating from birth which make marriage difficult.'

'But sir, these defects are certainly not real; why do you want me to be upset by them and why deprive your only daughter of the happiness she can find in marriage?'

'Have these ties made you very happy, madame?'

'Not all women make the mistakes which I have no doubt made, in failing to captivate you (and with a sigh), or else all husbands do not resemble you.'

'Wives . . . false, jealous, domineering, coquettish or pious . . . Husbands, treacherous, unfaithful, cruel or des-potic, there in a nutshell are all the individuals in the world, madame; don't hope to find a phoenix'.

'And yet everyone gets married.'

'Yes, the fools or the idlers; nobody ever marries, said one philosopher, except when they don't know what they are doing, or when they don't know what to do.'

'Must one let the world come to an end, then?'

'One might as well; it is never too early to exterminate a plant which yields nothing but poison.'

'Eugénie will not be very grateful to you for this excessive severity towards her.'

'Does this marriage appear to please her?'

'Your wishes are her commands, she said so.'

'Very well, madame, my wishes are that you give up this marriage.'

And Monsieur de Franval went out, again forbidding his wife in the strongest terms to speak of it again.

Madame de Franval did not fail to repeat to her mother the conversation she had just had with her husband, and Madame de Farneille, who was more subtle and more accustomed to the effects of the passions than her attractive daughter, suspected at once that there was something abnormal involved.

Eugénie very rarely saw her grandmother, for an hour at the most during social events, and always in Franval's presence. Madame de Farneille therefore, wishing to be enlightened, asked her son-in-law to send her granddaughter to her one day and leave her with her for a whole afternoon in order to cure her, she said, of an attack of migraine from which she was suffering; Franval replied harshly that there was nothing that Eugénie feared as much as the vapours, that he would however bring her where she was wanted but that she could not stay there long, since she was under an obligiation to go from there to a physics lesson, a course that she was following assiduously.

They went to Madame de Farneille's, who in no way concealed from her son-in-law her astonishment that the proposed marriage had been refused.

'I think,' she went on, 'you need have no fear in allowing your daughter to convince me herself of the defect which, according to you, must deprive her of marriage.'

'Whether this defect is real or not, madame,' said Franval somewhat surprised by his mother-in-law's determination, 'the fact is that it would cost me a great deal to marry my daughter and I am still too young to agree to such sacrifices; when she is twenty-five, she will do as she wishes; she must not count on me in any way until then.'

'And are your feelings still the same, Eugénie?' asked Madame de Farneille.

'They differ in one respect, madame,' said Mademoiselle de Franval very firmly; my father allows me to marry when I am twenty-five, and I, madame, assure both you and him that I will not take advantage at any point in my lifetime of a permission ... which, to my way of thinking, would only contribute to my unhappiness.'

'One has no way of thinking at your age, miss,' said Madame de Farneille, 'and there is something unusual in all this which I must certainly sort out.'

'I urge you to do so, madame,' said Franval, as he took his daughter away; 'it will even be a very good thing if you employ your clergy to penetrate to the heart of the problem, and when all your powers have exerted themselves cleverly, and when you finally know the answer, kindly tell me if I am right or wrong in opposing Eugénie's marriage.'

The sarcasm levelled by Franval at his mother-in-law's ecclesiastical advisers was aimed at a praiseworthy person whom it is relevant to introduce, since the progress of events will soon show him in action.

This was the spiritual director to Madame de Farneille and her daughter, one of the most virtuous men in France; honest, benevolent, straightforward and wise, Monsieur de Clervil, far from having all the vices of his cloth, possessed only gentle and useful qualities. A reliable support for the poor, a sincere friend of the opulent, consoler of the unfortunate, this worthy man had all the gifts which make someone likeable and all the virtues which make up a sensitive person.

When he was consulted Clervil replied like a man of good sense that before taking sides in this matter it was necessary to work out Monsieur de Franval's reasons for opposing his daughter's marriage; and although Madame de Farneille made some remarks likely to arouse suspicion about the intrigue which existed only too truly in fact, the prudent director rejected these ideas, and finding them much too insulting towards Madame de Franval and her husband, he disagreed with them indignantly.

'Crime is such a distressing thing, madame,' this honest man would sometimes say; 'it seems so unlikely that a well-conducted person will voluntarily exceed the bounds of modesty and all the restraints of virtue, that it is only with the most extreme repugnance that I decide to attribute such faults; let us only rarely suspect vice; such feelings are often the result of our *amour-propre*, almost always the outcome of a hidden comparison made in the depths of our mind; we hasten to admit evil so that we can be entitled to find ourselves better. If you think about it seriously, would it not be better, madame, if a secret fault were never laid bare, rather than for us to invent illusory ones through unforgivable haste and thus to blight without cause, as I see it, people who have committed no other errors except those which our pride has attributed to them? Moreover, does not everything gain from this principle? Is it not infinitely less essential to punish a crime than to prevent it from spreading? By leaving it in the obscurity it seeks, is it not as good as abolished? Scandal is certain to spread it abroad, descriptions of it arouse the passions of those inclined to the same type of errors; the inevitable blindness of crime arouses the hope of the guilty man to be happier than him who has just been recognised as such; he has not been given a lesson but a piece of advice, and he abandons himself to excesses that he would perhaps never have dared to commit without the imprudent scandal mistakenly regarded as justice ... and which is no more than ill-conceived severity or vanity in disguise.'

The only decision taken therefore at this first meeting was that of verifying precisely why Franval had put off his daughter's marriage, and why Eugénie shared the same way of thinking: it was decided that nothing should be undertaken before these motives were laid bare.

'Well, Eugénie,' said Franval that evening to his daughter, 'you see, they want to separate us, will they succeed, my child? Will they manage to sever the most cherished bonds of my life?'

'Never . . . never, do not fear it, my dearest friend! The ties in which you revel are as precious to me as to you; you have in no way deceived me, you showed me, while forming them, to what extent they clashed with custom; I am not afraid to contravene practices which, varying from one part of the world to another, cannot be sacred in any way; I desired these bonds, I wove them without remorse, do not fear therefore that I shall break them.'

'Alas, who knows? Colunce is younger than I am . . . He has everything necessary to attract you, do not heed, Eugénie, the residue of error which no doubt blinds you; maturity and the light of reason will dispel prestige and will soon lead to regrets, you will blame me for them, and I shall not forgive myself for having been the cause of them!'

'No,' Eugénie went on firmly, 'no, I am determined to love you alone; I should believe myself the most unfortunate of women if I had to take a husband . . . I,' she went on, with warmth, 'link myself to a stranger who, not having like you twin reasons for loving me, would limit his feelings, at the most his desires . . . If I were to be abandoned and despised by him, what would become of me afterwards? Would I be a sanctimonious prude or a harlot? Oh, no, no, I would rather be your mistress, my friend. Yes, I love you a thousand times too much to be reduced to playing in society either of those infamous roles . . . But what is the cause of all this disturbance?' Eugénie went on bitterly. . . . 'Do you know what it is, my friend? Who it is? Your wife! She alone . . . Her insatiable jealousy . . . Have no doubt about it, those are the sole causes of the misfortunes which threaten us . . . Ah! I do not blame her for it: everything is simple . . . everything is understandable . . . everything is possible when it is a question of keeping you. What would I not undertake if I were in her place, and someone wanted to take your heart away from me?'

Franval, strangely moved, embraced his daughter time and time again; and the latter, further encouraged by these criminal caresses, developing her atrocious thoughts in a more energetic fashion, dared to tell her father, with unpardonable shamelessness, that the only way in which they could both be less closely observed was to provide her mother with a lover. This plan entertained Franval; but since he was much more wicked than his daughter and wanted imperceptibly to prepare her youthful heart for all the feelings of hatred against his wife that he intended to sow there, he replied that he thought this revenge too mild, and that there were many other ways of upsetting a woman when she annoyed her husband.

A few weeks passed in this manner, during which Franval and his daughter finally decided on the first plan conceived to bring despair to this monster's virtuous wife, believing, rightly, that before adopting more unworthy procedures, they must at least try to produce a lover; this would not only provide material for all other methods, but, if it succeeded, would of necessity oblige Madame de Franval not to concern herself with the faults of others, since her own would also have been revealed. In order to carry out this project Franval examined all the young men of his acquaintance and, after thinking things over carefully, he found that only Valmont seemed likely to prove useful to him.

Valmont was thirty years old, handsome, witty, imaginative, with no principles whatever, and as a result highly suitable for the role that was to be offered to him. Franval invited him to dinner one evening, and as they left the table he took him aside.

'My friend,' he said, 'I have always deemed you to be worthy of me; now is the moment to prove that I have not been mistaken: I demand a proof of your feelings . . . but a very unusual proof.'

'What is all this? Explain yourself, dear man, and never doubt my anxiety to serve you!'

'What do you think of my wife?'

'She is delightful; and if you were not her husband, I'd have been her lover for a long time.'

'That is a most considerate remark, Valmont, but it does not move me.'

'Why not?'

'I'm going to surprise you . . . it is precisely because you like me, precisely because I am Madame de Franval's husband that I demand you to become her lover.'

'Are you mad?'

'No, but I'm whimsical . . . capricious, you've known me to be like this for a long time . . . I want virtue to come to grief and I would like it to be you who takes her in the snare.'

'What an outrageous idea!'

'Don't say a word, this is a masterpiece of reasoning.'

'What! You want me to . . . ?'

'Yes, I want it, I demand it, and I cease to regard you as my friend if you refuse me this favour . . . I will look after you . . . I will satisfy all your needs . . . it will be to your advantage; and, as soon as I am quite certain of my fate, I shall, if necessary, throw myself at your feet to thank you for obliging me.'

'Franval, you cannot deceive me; there is something very unusual in all this . . . I will undertake nothing unless I know everything.'

'Yes . . . but I think you have some scruples, I suspect that you aren't yet intelligent enough to be capable of understanding all that is involved. . . . You still have prejudices, you're still chivalrous, I wager? You will shudder like a child when I've told you everything, and you won't want to do anything any more.'

'I, shudder? I am really amazed at your way of judging me: learn, my dear friend, that there is not an aberration in the world . . . not a single one, however irregular it might be, that is capable of upsetting me for a moment.'

'Valmont, have you cast eyes on Eugénie?'

'Your daughter?'

'Or my mistress, if you prefer?'

'Ah, you scoundrel, I understand you.'

'That's the first time in my life I've found you to be intelligent.'

'What is this? Tell me honestly, are you in love with your daughter?'

'Yes, my friend, like Lot! I have always had such a great respect for the holy scriptures, I was always so convinced that one could gain heaven by emulating their heroes! Ah, my friend, the madness of Pygmalion no longer surprises me . . . is the universe not full of these weaknesses? Was it not necessary to start in this way in order to populate the world? And if it was not evil then, can it have become so since? How preposterous! May not a pretty woman attract me because I made the mistake of bringing her into the world? Should the thing which ought to link me to her more closely become the reason for separating me from her? Should I look at her coldly because she resembles me, because she is my own flesh and blood, because in her are united every foundation for the most ardent love? . . . Ah, what sophistries . . . how ridiculous! Let us leave to fools these absurd restraints, they are not made for souls like ours; the dominion of beauty and the sacred rights of love know nothing of futile human conventions; their ascendancy annihilates these just as the rays of the sun purify the earth from the fogs that enshroud her at night. Let us trample underfoot these atrocious prejudices which have always been hostile to happiness; if they sometimes prevailed over reason, it was only at the expense of the most seductive pleasures . . . let us despise them for ever.'

'You convince me,' replied Valmont, 'and I completely agree that your Eugénie must be a delightful mistress; she is a more lively beauty than her mother, and if she does not possess, like your wife, quite that languor which takes hold of the heart in such a voluptuous way, she has that piquancy which overwhelms us, which seems in fact to subdue every possibility of resistance; if the mother appears to yield, the daughter demands; what the former permits, the latter offers, and I find this much more attractive.'

'Yet I am giving you not Eugénie, but her mother.'

'Now what reason leads you to do this?'

'My wife is jealous, she gets in my way, she criticises me, she wants to arrange a marriage for Eugénie, I must make her have faults in order to conceal my own; therefore you must have her . . . amuse yourself with her for some time . . and betray her afterwards . . . I must surprise you in her arms . . . punish her, or through this discovery I must

purchase peace on both sides in our mutual errors . . .
but no love, Valmont, keep cool, enslave her, and don't let
yourself be dominated; if feelings come into it, my plans
will be wrecked.'

'Have no fear, this would be the first time a woman has
moved me.'

Our two scoundrels therefore concluded their arrangements, and it was resolved that within a few days Valmont
would take Madame de Franval in hand, with full permission to do everything he wanted to achieve success . . .
even the avowal of Franval's love, as the most powerful
means of making this honest woman decide on revenge.

Eugénie, to whom the plan was confided, found it vastly
entertaining; the infamous creature dared to say that if
Valmont succeeded it was necessary, if her own happiness
were to be as complete as possible, for her to be assured,
through her own eyes, of her mother's downfall, for her to
see this virtuous heroine yield incontestably to the pleasur-
able delights which she condemned with such severity.

Finally came the day when the most demure and unfortunate of women was not only to receive the most
painful blow that could be dealt her, but was to be sufficiently outraged by her frightful husband to be abandoned
. . . delivered by him to the man by whom he consented to
be dishonoured . . . What madness! What scorn of all
principles! For what purpose can nature create hearts as
depraved as these? A few preliminary conversations had set
this scene; Valmont, moreover, was friendly enough with
Franval for the latter's wife, to whom this had already
happened without risk, to be incapable of imagining that
any danger would be incurred by remaining alone with
him. They were all three in the drawing-room, when Franval
rose.

'I must leave,' he said, 'an important business matter
calls me . . . It's like putting you with your governess,
madame,' he added with a laugh, 'leaving you with Valmont, he's so well behaved . . . but if he forgets himself,
you must tell me, I don't like him enough yet to hand over
my rights to him. . . .'

And the shameless man went out.

After a few commonplace remarks, arising from Franval's joke, Valmont said that he had found his friend changed during the last six months.

'I have not dared to ask him why,' he went on, 'but he seems unhappy.'

'What is very certain,' replied Madame de Franval, 'is the terrible unhappiness he is causing to others.'

'Oh heavens, what are you telling me? Has my friend been treating you badly?'

'If only that were the extent of our troubles!'

'Do please tell me, you know my ardour, my undying attachment.'

'A series of horrible disturbances . . . moral corruption, in fact errors of all kinds . . . would you believe it? The most advantageous marriage is suggested to us on behalf of our daughter . . . he does not want it . . .'

And at this point the skilful Valmont looked away, with the air of a man who understands . . . groans . . . and dare not explain himself.

'How is this, sir?' went on Madame de Franval, 'are you not astonished by what I am saying? Your silence is very strange.'

'Ah, madame, is it not better to be silent than to say something that would bring despair to the person one loves?'

'What is this enigma, explain yourself, I entreat you.'

'How can I not shudder at opening your eyes,' said Valmont, impetuously seizing this charming woman's hand.

'Oh sir,' went on Madame de Franval with much animation, 'either say not another word, or explain yourself, I insist . . . you are putting me in a terrible position.'

'Much less so perhaps than the state to which you reduce me yourself,' said Valmont, looking at the woman he was trying to seduce, his eyes ablaze with love.

'But what does all this mean, sir? You begin by alarming me, you make me want an explanation, next you dare to let me hear things which I should not and cannot tolerate, you remove from me the means of learning from you what torments me so cruelly. Speak, sir, speak, or you will reduce me to despair.'

'I shall be less obscure then, since you demand it, madame, and although it costs me something to break your heart . . . learn the harsh reason for your husband's refusal to Monsieur de Colunce . . . Eugénie . . .'

'Well?'

'Well, madame, Franval adores her; he is now not so much her father as her lover, and he would prefer to stop living rather than give up Eugénie.'

Madame de Franval did not hear this fatal explanation without a shock which made her lose her senses; Valmont hastened to go to her aid.

'You see, madame,' he went on, 'the cost of the avowal that you demanded . . . Not for anything in the world would I . . .'

'Leave me, sir, leave me,' said Madame de Franval, in a state difficult to describe; 'after such violent shocks I need to be alone for a moment.'

'And would you want me to leave you in this state? I feel your sorrows too vividly in my heart not to ask your permission to share them. I inflicted this wound, let me heal it.'

'Franval in love with his daughter, gracious heaven! This creature whom I bore within me, it is she who rends his heart in such atrocious style! Such a fearful crime . . . ah, sir, is it possible? Are your really sure?'

'If I still had doubts about it, madame, I would have kept silence, I would have preferred a hundred times to tell you nothing rather than upset you to no purpose; it was from your husband himself that I received proof of this infamy, he confided it to me; however that may be, be calm, I beg you; let us concern ourselves now with the means of breaking this intrigue rather than with those for explaining it; now, these means rest only with you. . . .'

'Ah, tell me about them quickly . . . this crime horrifies me.'

'A husband with Franval's character, madame, is not won back in any way by virtue; your husband has little faith in the sage demeanour of women; he maintains that it is due to their pride or their temperament, the things they do to preserve themselves for us are done much more to satisfy themselves than to please or enslave us. . . . Forgive me, madame, but I will not disguise from you that I believe more or less as he does on this subject; I never saw that virtues made a wife succeed in destroying her husband's vices; conduct more or less similar to Franval's would rouse him much more and would bring him back to you much more satisfactorily; jealousy would certainly result, and how many hearts have been restored to love through this constantly infallible method; your husband, then, seeing that this virtue, to which he is accustomed, and which he has the effrontery to despise, is due much more to reflection than to carelessness, will really learn to appreciate it in you, at the moment when he believes you capable of failing in it; . . . he imagines, he dares to say that if you have never had any lovers it is because you have never been attacked; prove to him that it only depends on you to be so . . . to have your revenge for his wrongs and his scorn; perhaps you will do a little harm, in view of your stern principles, but how many evils you will have prevented; what a husband you will have converted! And for a slight outrage to the goddess you revere, what a worshipper you will have brought back to her temple! Ah, madame, I appeal only to your reason. Through the conduct that I dare recommend to you, you will bring Franval back for ever, you will captivate him for good; he flees through contrariness, he is escaping for good; yes, madame, I dare to say it, either you do not love your husband, or you must not hesitate.'

Madame de Franval, who was very surprised by these words, did not reply for some time; then she spoke, recalling Valmont's looks and his first remarks.

'Sir,' she said skilfully, 'supposing that I take the advice you give me, on whom do you think I should cast my eyes in order to upset my husband more?'

'Ah!' cried Valmont, not seeing the trap that was being set for him, 'dear, divine friend . . . on the man who loves you best in all the world, on him who has adored you ever since he has known you, and who swears on his knees that he will die in your service . . .'

'Go, sir, go!' said Madame de Franval then in imperious fashion, 'and never appear before me again; your trick is exposed; you only credit my husband with faults . . . that he is incapable of possessing in order to arrange your treacherous seduction more successfully; understand that even if he were guilty, the methods you suggest to me would be too repugnant for me to use them for one moment; a husband's errors can never justify those of a wife; for her they should become additional reasons for good conduct, so that the just and eternal God may find them in the afflicted cities that are about to suffer the effects of his anger, and may, if he can, turn aside from them the flames that are about to devour them.'

With these words Madame de Franval went out, and, asking for Valmont's servants, she obliged him to leave . . . very much ashamed of the first steps that he had taken.

Although this attractive woman had seen through the tricks of Franval's friend, the things he had said corresponded so well with her own fears and with those of her mother, that she decided to put everything into operation in order to convince herself of these hurtful truths. She went to see Madame de Farneille, told her what had happened and came back, determined to proceed as follows.

It has long been said, and very rightly so, that we have no greater enemies than our own servants; they are always jealous and envious and apparently try to lighten their burdens by attributing faults to us which place us beneath them and allow their vanity, for a short time at least, to dominate us in the way that fate has denied to them.

Madame de Franval had one of Eugénie's women bribed; a guaranteed payment, a pleasant future, the semblance of a good action, everything influenced this minion and she undertook, from the following night, to put Madame de Franval in a position where she would be unable to doubt her misfortune any longer.

The moment came. The unfortunate mother was introduced into a small room adjoining the apartment where every night her faithless husband violated both his own marriage ties and Heaven too. Eugénie was with her father; several candles still burned in a corner to illuminate the crime . . . the altar was prepared, the victim took her place, the high priest followed her . . . Madame de Franval no longer had any support except her despair, her angry love, her courage . . . She broke through the doors that held her back and rushed into the apartment; there she fell on her knees before the incestuous man.

'Oh,' she cried, addressing Franval, 'you are breaking my heart, I did not deserve such treatment from you . . . you whom I still adore, whatever insults I receive from you, see my tears . . . and do not reject me; I ask you to spare this unfortunate girl, who, deceived by her weakness and seduced by you, believes she is finding happiness in the midst of shame and crime. . . . Eugénie, Eugénie, do you want to thrust a sword into the bosom that gave you life? No longer be the accomplice in a crime whose horror is concealed from you! Come, hasten, my arms are ready to receive you. See your unfortunate mother, on her knees before you, begging you not to outrage both honour and nature at once. . . . But if you refuse me both,' went on the heartbroken woman, raising a dagger to her heart, 'this is the means by which I shall remove myself from the hurt you are trying to inflict upon me; I will spatter you with my blood and it is only over my wretched body that you will be able to consummate your crimes.'

That Franval's hardened soul could resist this sight, those who are beginning to know this scoundrel will easily believe; but that Eugénie did not yield in any way is inconceivable.

'Madame,' said this corrupt girl, with the most harsh indifference, 'I do not regard it as reasonable on your part, I confess, that you should make an absurd scene in front of your husband; can he not do as he pleases? And if he approves of what I do, have you any right to criticise? Do we criticise your indiscretions with Monsieur de Valmont? Do we disturb your pleasures? Kindly respect ours, therefore, or do not be surprised that I am the first to press your husband to take the line which could force you to do so.'

At this moment Madame de Franval lost patience, all her anger turned against this unworthy creature who could forget herself so far as to speak to her like this, and, rising in a fury, she hurled herself upon her. . . . But the hateful, cruel Franval, seizing his wife by the hair, dragged her in fury far away from his daughter and from the bedroom, and threw her forcefully down the stairs of the house, until she fell faint and bleeding at the door of one of her women who, awakened by the horrible noise, hastily removed her mistress from the furies of the tyrannical Franval, who had already come down in order to despatch his unfortunate victim . . . She was taken to her rooms, locked in and cared for, while the monster, who had just treated her with such rage, rushed back to his detestable companion to spend the night as quietly as though he had not sunk lower than the fiercest beasts, through crimes so execrable, so likely to humiliate him . . . so horrible in fact that we blush at the necessity to reveal them.

No more illusions for the unfortunate Madame de Franval; she could no longer allow herself a single one; it was only too obvious that her husband's heart, that is to say the dearest possession of her life, had been taken away from her . . . and by whom? By her who owed her the greatest respect . . . and who had just spoken to her with the greatest insolence; she had also suspected that the whole of the Valmont intrigue was merely a horrible trap for the purpose of putting her in the wrong if possible, and, if not, to attribute faults to her, to inundate her with them, in order to balance and justify thereby the infinitely more serious ones which others dared to incur against her.

Nothing was more certain. Franval, informed of Valmont's failure, had pledged him to replace truth by imposture and indiscretion . . . to spread the story that he was Madame de Franval's lover; and it had been concluded that disgusting letters would be faked which would prove, in the least equivocal manner, the existence of the relationship to which this unfortunate wife had refused to lend herself.

Madame de Franval however, who was in despair, and even suffering from several injuries, fell seriously ill; her barbarous husband, who refused to see her, not even deigning to enquire about her health, left with Eugénie for the country, on the pretext that there was fever in the house and he did not wish to expose his daughter to it.

Valmont presented himself several times at Madame de Franval's door during her illness, but without being admitted once; closeted with her loving mother and Monsieur de Clervil, she saw nobody whatsoever; consoled by such dear friends, who were accustomed to have authority over her, she was restored to life by their care and after six weeks was in a state to see people. Franval then brought his daughter back to Paris and made arrangements with Valmont to provide themselves with weapons equal to those which Madame de Franval and her friends seemed about to level against them.

The villainous Franval went to see his wife as soon as he believed her to be in a fit state to receive him.

'Madame,' he said to her coldly, 'you should have no doubts about the consideration I have shown over your health; I cannot disguise from you the fact that this alone is responsible for Eugénie's reticence; she had decided to bring the strongest charges against you concerning the way in which you treated her; however convinced she may be of the respect which a daughter owes to her mother, she cannot all the same be unaware that the mother puts herself in the worst possible position by hurling herself upon her daughter with a dagger in her hand; hastiness of this kind, madame, could open the eyes of the government to your conduct and one day could not fail to cause injury to your liberty and your honour.'

'I did not expect this recrimination, sir,' replied Madame de Franval; 'and when my daughter, seduced by you, renders herself simultaneously guilty of incest, adultery, licentiousness and the most hateful ingratitude towards her who brought her into the world . . . yes, I admit, I did not imagine that after this complex of horrors it would be for me to fear complaints: all your artifice and evil are required, sir, to excuse the crime with such audacity and accuse an innocent person.'

'I am not unaware, madame, that the pretexts for your scene were the odious suspicions that your dare to form about me, but fantasies do not justify crimes; what you thought is false, but what you have done is unfortunately only too real. You are surprised at the reproaches that my daughter addressed to you concerning your irregular conduct only after the whole of Paris has done so; this state of affairs is so well known ... the proofs are unfortunately so consistent, that those who speak about it are guilty at the most of imprudence but not of calumny.'

'I, sir,' said this honourable wife, rising indignantly, 'I, an intrigue with Valmont? Gracious heavens, and you say that!' She burst into tears. 'Ungrateful man! This is the price of my affection ... this is the reward for having loved you so much: you are not content with outraging me so cruelly, it is not enough for you to seduce my own daughter, you must still dare to justify your crimes by attributing to me others which I regard as more terrible than death...' She collected herself again: 'You have proofs of this intrigue sir, you say, bring them out, I demand that they be made public, I will force you to show them to everyone, if you refuse to show them to me.'

'No, madame, I shall certainly not show them to everyone, a husband does not usually announce things of this kind; he bewails them and hides them as carefully as he can; but if *you* demand them, madame, I will certainly not refuse them to you ...' He then took a wallet out of his pocket. 'Be seated,' he said, 'this must be verified with calm, excitement and anger would do harm without convincing me; compose yourself then, I beg you, and let us discuss this coolly.'

Madame de Franval, who was perfectly convinced of her innocence, did not know what to think of these preparations and her surprise, mingled with fear, kept her in a state of frenzy.

'First of all, madame,' said Franval, emptying one side of the wallet, 'here is your entire correspondence with Valmont during the last six months or so. Do not accuse this young man of imprudence or indiscretion: he is no doubt too honourable to dare fail you on this point. But one of his servants, whose skill exceeds his master's attentiveness, found the secret of procuring for me these precious monuments to your exemplary conduct and your eminent virtue.' He fingered the letters which he scattered on the table.

'Allow me,' he went on, 'to select from much of the usual chatter of a woman who is excited . . . by a very attractive man one letter which seemed to me more abandoned and even more decisive than the others . . . Here it is, madame:

' "My tedious husband is taking supper this evening at his *petite maison* in the outer part of the town with that horrible creature . . . whom it is impossible I brought into the world; come, my dear, and console me for all the sorrows that those two monsters cause me. . . . What am I saying? are they not rendering me the greatest possible service at present, and will not this intrigue prevent my husband from noticing ours? Let him then tighten the knots as far as he wishes, but may he not attempt at least to sever those which link me to the only man I have really adored in all the world."

'Well, madame?'

'Well, sir, I admire you,' replied Madame de Franval; 'every day adds to the incredible esteem that you deserve; and whatever great qualities I had recognised in you so far, I admit I did not yet know you possessed those of forger and calumniator.'

'Are you denying it, then?'

'Not at all; I only ask to be convinced; we will have judges appointed . . . experts, and if you agree, shall we ask for the most severe penalty to be inflicted on whichever one of us shall be found guilty?'

'That is what is called effrontery: well, I prefer that to sorrow. . . . Let us proceed. That you have a lover, madame,' said Franval, shaking the other part of the wallet, 'with your pretty face and "tedious husband", nothing could be simpler, certainly; but that at your age you should keep this lover, and at my expense, is something you may allow me to find not so simple. . . . However, here are notes of hand, or accounts paid by you, or signed by you, on behalf of Valmont, amounting to 100,000 écus; kindly glance through them, I entreat you,' added this monster, showing them to her without letting her touch them. . . .

> To Zaide, jeweller.
> Signed, the attached note for the sum of twenty-two thousand livres on behalf of Monsieur de Valmont, by arrangement with him.
>
> FARNEILLE DE FRANVAL

'To Jamet, horse dealer, *six thousand livres* . . . that is the brown bay team which is today the delight of Valmont and the admiration of all Paris . . . Yes, madame, there are sums amounting to *three hundred thousand two hundred and eighty-three livres ten sols,* of which you still owe more than a third, and of which you have very honourably paid the rest . . . Well, madame?'

'Oh, sir, this fraud is too clumsy to cause me the slightest concern; I demand only one thing to confound those who invent these things against me . . . that the people to whom I have allegedly paid these accounts come forward, and that they swear I have had dealings with them.'

'They will do so, madame, have no doubt about it; would they have informed me themselves of your conduct if they were not determined to uphold their declarations? One of them was even going to sue you today, unless I had intervened. . . .'

Bitter tears then sprang to this unhappy woman's beautiful eyes; her courage no longer sustained her, she collapsed in sudden despair, mingled with frightening symptoms, she struck her head against the marble pillars that surrounded her and bruised her face.

'Sir,' she cried, throwing herself at her husband's feet, 'kindly rid yourself of me, I beg you, by means that are less slow and less frightful; since my existence restricts your life of crime, destroy it at one blow . . . do not plunge me into the tomb so slowly. . . . Am I guilty for having loved you? For having turned against that which took your heart away from me so cruelly? Well, then, punish me for it, barbarian, yes, take this weapon,' she said, hurling herself upon her husband's sword, 'take it, I tell you, and pierce my bosom without mercy; but at least let me die deserving your esteem, let me carry to the tomb, as my sole consolation, the certainty that you believe me incapable of the infamous crimes of which you accuse me . . . that in order to conceal your own . . .'

And she was on her knees, lying at Franval's feet, her hands bleeding and hurt by the naked blade which she attempted to seize in order to rend her bosom asunder; this beautiful bosom was bared, her hair fell over it in disorder and was drenched by her copious tears; never did sorrow look more pathetic and expressive, never had it been more touching, more attractive and more noble.

'No, madame,' said Franval, opposing her gesture, 'it is not your death that is required, but your punishment; I understand your repentance, your tears in no way astonish me, you are furious at being found out; these attitudes of yours please me, they make me prophesy an improvement . . . which will be precipitated no doubt by the fate to which I destine you; I hasten to give it attention.'

'Stop, Franval,' cried the unhappy woman, 'do not noise your dishonour abroad, do not tell the public yourself that you are guilty of perjury, forgery, incest and calumny. . . . You wish to be rid of me, I shall flee you, I shall seek out some resting place where even your memory shall escape me . . . you will be free, you will commit crimes with impunity . . . yes, I shall forget you . . . if I can, cruel man, or if your heart-rending image cannot be effaced from my heart, if it still pursues me in my remote obscurity . . . I shall not efface it, faithless man, that would be beyond me, no, I shall not efface it, but I shall punish myself for my blindness, and I shall then confine within the horror of the tomb the guilty body that loved you too much. . . .'

At these words, the last outbursts of a soul exhausted by illness, the unfortunate woman fainted and fell unconscious. The cold shadows of death spread over her beautiful skin, which was already wasted by despair; she was no more than a lifeless mass, although it was impossible for the grace, modesty and all the charms of virtue to abandon her. The monster went out, on his way to enjoy, with his guilty daughter, the frightful triumph that vice, or rather the wicked girl, dared to win over innocence and misfortune.

These details gave infinite pleasure to the execrable Eugénie, who would have liked to see all this herself ... the horror should have been carried further, Valmont should have triumphed over her mother's severity, Franval should have surprised them making love. If all this had happened, what means of self-justification would have been left to their victim? And was it not important to remove them all from her? That was what Eugénie was like.

However, Franval's unfortunate wife, who could only confide in her mother, soon told her about her new reasons for sorrow; it was then that Madame de Farneille imagined that the age, status and personal reputation of Monsieur de Clervil might perhaps have some good influence on her son-in-law; there is nothing so trusting as misfortune; she informed the worthy ecclesiastic as best she could of all Franval's licentiousness, she convinced him of what he had never wanted to believe, she enjoined him most of all to use with such a villain only that persuasive eloquence which is more suited to the heart than to the mind; she recommended that after talking to the perfidious man he should obtain an interview with Eugénie, when he would employ all the most likely means to explain to this unfortunate young woman the abyss that yawned at her feet, and to bring her back, if possible, to her mother and to virtue.

Franval, learning that Clervil was to ask if he could see his daughter and himself, had time to devise a scheme with her, and as soon as their plans were made, they let Madame de Farneille's director know that they were both ready to hear him. The credulous Madame de Franval hoped that the eloquence of this spiritual guide would achieve everything; unfortunate people seize hold of fantasies so avidly, and in order to find the pleasures denied to them by reality, they achieve with much art all possible illusions.

Clervil arrived: it was nine o'clock in the morning; Franval received him in the apartment where he was accustomed to spending the nights with his daughter; he had had it decorated with all imaginable elegance, while leaving all the same a kind of disorder which revealed his criminal pleasures ... Eugénie, who was nearby, could hear everything, so that she could be better prepared for the interview to which she was destined in her turn.

'It is only with the greatest fear of disturbing you, sir,' said Clervil, 'that I dare to present myself before you; persons of my calling are usually so burdensome to people who like you spend their lives in the pleasures of this world, that I reproach myself with having agreed to the wishes of Madame de Farneille and asking permission to talk to you for a moment.'

'Sit down, sir, and as long as you speak the language of justice and reason, never fear that you are causing me annoyance.'

'You are adored by a young wife full of charm and virtue, and you are accused, sir, of making her very unhappy; since she has on her side only her innocence and lack of guile, since she has only her mother to listen to her complaints, and since she worships you still in spite of your faults, you can easily imagine the horror of her situation!'

'I would like us to get to the point, sir, it seems to me that you are beating about the bush; what is the object of your mission?'

'To make you both happy again, if possible.'

'Therefore, if I am happy as I am, you will have nothing more to say to me?'

'It is impossible, sir, to find happiness in crime.'

'I agree; but he who, through profound study and mature reflection has been able to achieve a state of mind in which he suspects no evil in anything and can see all human actions with the most calm indifference, considering them all the necessary results of some kind of power, which, sometimes benevolent and sometimes perverse, but always authoritarian, inspires us in turn to actions which men either approve or condemn, but never anything which upsets or disturbs it—you will agree, sir, that a man can be equally happy, behaving as I do, as you are in the career you pursue: happiness is an abstraction, it is a product of the imagination; it is a way of being moved, which depends entirely on our way of seeing and feeling; apart from the satisfaction of our needs, there is no one way of making all men equally happy; every day we see one individual become happy through something which is totally displeasing to another; there is therefore no certain happiness, no other can exist for us except that which we make for ourselves as a result of our constitutions and our principles!'

'I know, sir, but if the mind deceives us, conscience never leads us astray, and that is the book in which nature inscribes all our duties.'

'And do we not do as we wish with this artificial conscience? Habit modifies it, conscience for us is like pliable wax which assumes all shapes in our hands; if this book were as infallible as you say, would man not have an unvarying conscience? From one end of the world to the other would all actions not be the same for him? And yet is that the case? Does the Hottentot tremble at what frightens the Frenchman? And does not the latter do things every day which would cause him to be punished in Japan? No, sir, no, there is nothing real in the world, nothing which merits praise or blame, nothing which deserves to be rewarded or punished, nothing that is not unjust in one place and legitimate five hundred leagues away, no real evil, in fact no constant good.'

'Do not believe it, sir, virtue is not an illusion; it is not a question of knowing whether something is good in one place or bad a few degrees away, in order to define it precisely as crime or virtue, and to be certain of finding happiness in it as a result of one's choice; the sole happiness of man can only lie in the most complete submission to the laws of his country; he must either respect them or be wretched, there is no middle way between infringement of them and unhappiness. It is not, if you like, from these things in themselves that spring the evils that overwhelm us: when we abandon ourselves to them, when they are forbidden, it is the harm that these things, good or bad in themselves, cause to the social conventions of the region we inhabit. There is certainly nothing wrong in preferring to walk on the boulevards rather than in the Champs-Elysées; if, nevertheless, a law were promulgated which forbade the boulevards to the citizens, he who infringed this law would perhaps lay up a never-ending sequence of misfortunes for himself, although he would only have done something very simple in breaking it: the habit moreover of breaking ordinary laws soon leads to the breaking of more important ones, and from one mistake to another a man comes to crimes which are punished in every country of the world, made to inspire fright in all the reasonable creatures who inhabit the globe, in either hemisphere. If there is not a universal conscience for mankind, there is therefore a national one, relative to the existence we have received from nature, and where her hand traces our duties in characters that we cannot erase without danger. For example, sir, your family accuses you of incest; whatever sophistries may have been used to justify this crime and mitigate its horrors, however specious the reasonings undertaken on this question, whatever support may have been given to them by examples taken from neighbouring countries, it has nevertheless been proved that this crime, which is not one among certain races, is definitely dangerous in countries where it is forbidden by law; it is none the less true that it can lead to the most dire consequences, and crimes made necessary by this first crime, crimes, I repeat, which are the most likely to inspire horror in mankind. If you had married your daughter on the banks of the Ganges, where such marriages are permitted, you might have committed a very inferior form of evil; under a government which forbids these alliances, by offering this revolting spectacle to the public . . . to a wife who adores you, and who is being driven to her grave by this treachery, you are undoubtedly committing a shocking action, a crime which is tending to break the most sacred links of nature, those which, attaching your daughter to the being from whom she received life, should make this man for her the most worthy of respect and the most sacred of all people. You are forcing this girl to despise duties which are just as vital, you are making her hate the person who bore her within her womb; without realising it you are preparing weapons which she can direct against you; you are presenting no system of thought to her, you are instilling into her no principles by which you are not condemned; and if one day she threatens to take your life, then you yourself will have sharpened the dagger.'

'Your manner of reasoning,' replied Franval, 'so different from that used by people of your calling, will in the first place incline me towards confidence, sir; I could deny your accusation; my frankness in unmasking myself before you will oblige you, I hope, to believe equally in the wrong-doings of my wife, when I employ, in order to describe them to you, the same truth that will direct the avowal of mine. Yes, sir, I love my daughter, she is my mistress, my wife, my sister, my confidante, my friend, my only god on earth, she has in fact all the rights which can win the homage of the heart, and all mine is due to her; these feelings will last as long as my life; I must therefore justify them, no doubt, since I cannot succeed in renouncing them.'

'A father's first duty towards his daughter is undoubtedly, you will agree, sir, to make her as happy as possible; if he does not succeed in this, he has failed her; if he succeeds, he is protected from all reproaches. I have neither seduced nor forced Eugénie, this consideration is worthy of note, do not forget it; I have in no way concealed the world from her, I have described to her the roses of marriage alongside the thorns that people find within it; I offered myself afterwards, I left Eugénie free to choose, she had plenty of time for reflection; she did not hesitate in any way, she protested that she found happiness only with me; was I wrong in giving her, in order to make her happy, that which, with full knowledge of the facts, she seemed to prefer to anything else?'

(48)

'These sophistries do not justify anything, sir; you should not let your daughter see that the being whom she could not prefer without being guilty could become the object of her happiness; however fine a fruit might appear, would you not repent of offering it to someone if you were sure that death lurked within its flesh? No, sir, no, you have considered only yourself in this unfortunate behaviour, and you have made your daughter both accomplice and victim; these actions are forgivable . . . and this virtuous and sensitive wife, whose bosom you tear asunder at your pleasure, what wrongs has she done in your eyes, what wrongs, unjust man . . . beyond that of worshipping you?'

'That is what I wanted to ask, sir, and it is on this point that I expect you to trust me; I have no doubt some right to hope for this, after the very frank way in which you have seen me agree to the accusations made against me!'

Franval then showed Clervil the forged letters and notes that he had attributed to his wife, assuring him that nothing was more genuine than these papers and Madame Franval's intrigue with the man to whom they were addressed.

Clervil knew everything.

'Well, sir,' he then said firmly to Franval, 'was I right to tell you that an error regarded at first as harmless can, by accustoming us to go beyond the limits, lead us to the worst excesses of crime and evil? You began by an action which seems to you of no import, and you see all the infamies that it can cause you to commit in order to justify it or conceal it. . . . Believe me, sir, let us throw these unforgivable slanderous documents into the fire and forget them utterly, I entreat you.'

'These papers are genuine, sir.'

'They are false.'

'You can only be in doubt; is that enough to contradict me?'

'Allow me, sir; I have only your word that they are genuine, and it is very much in your interest to uphold your accusation; my belief that these papers are false rests on the statements of your wife, and it would also be very much in her interest, if they were genuine, for her to tell me so; that is how I see the matter, sir. . . . Self-interest lies behind all that men do, forming the important motive for all their actions; wherever I find this, the torch of truth shines for me; this rule has never deceived me, I have followed it for forty years; and besides, would not your wife's virtue abolish this dreadful calumny for all to see? Would anyone, with her frankness, her candour, with the ardent love that she still has for you, allow herself such atrocious behaviour? No, sir, no, those are by no means the starting-points of crime; since you are so well acquainted with the results, you should know better how to direct the motives.'

'This is invective, sir!'

'Forgive me, injustice, calumny and licentious behaviour revolt me to such an extent that I cannot always control the agitation into which these horrors plunge me; let us burn these papers, sir, I again entreat you to do so . . . let us burn them, for the sake of your honour and peace of mind.'

'I did not imagine, sir,' said Franval, rising, 'that anyone exercising your ministry could so easily become the apologist and protector of misconduct and adultery; my wife is blighting my reputation, she is ruining me, I can prove it to you; you are so blind concerning her that you prefer to accuse me instead and would rather regard me as a calumniator than see her as a faithless and debauched wife! Well, sir, the law will decide; all the courts in France will ring with my accusations, I will take them all my proofs, I will make public the dishonour I am suffering, and then we shall see whether you will still be kind or rather stupid enough to protect such a shameless creature against me.'

'I shall withdraw, then, sir,' said Clervil, rising also; 'I did not imagine that the perverseness of your mind would cause such a deterioration in the qualities of your heart, and that, blinded by unjust revenge, you would become capable of supporting in cold blood things that could lead to madness. . . . Ah, sir, how all this convinces me more than ever that when a man has failed in the most sacred of his

duties, he immediately allows himself to abolish all the
others. . . . If on reflection you change your mind, condescend to let me know, sir, and you will always find in your
family and in me friends ready to accept you. . . . Am I
allowed to see your daughter for a moment?'

'You may, sir, I even exhort you to prevail over her
either by more eloquent methods or more effective resources
in order to present her with these luminous truths in which
I have had the misfortune to see only blindness and
sophistries.'

Clervil went into Eugénie's apartments. She was waiting
for him, clad in the most seductive and most elegant
déshabillé; a similar indecency, due to self-indulgence and
crime, reigned shamelessly in her looks and gestures, and
the perfidious girl, outraging the graces which beautified
her in spite of herself, personified all those that enflame
vice and repulse virtue.

Since it is not fitting for a young girl to enter into the
profound details as a *philosophe* like Franval, Eugénie
restricted herself to superficialities; gradually she reached
the stage of extreme provocation; but she soon saw that her
seductive arts were wasted and that a man as virtuous as
this could not be caught in her toils, she skilfully loosened
the clothes which concealed her charms, and appeared in
the greatest disorder before Clervil had time to notice it.

'The wretch!' she cried loudly, 'take this monster away!
And in particular conceal his crime from my father. Good
heavens! I expect pious advice from him . . . and the
dishonourable man attacks my modesty . . . See,' she said
to her servants who came running as she cried out, 'see in
what state this shameless man has put me; so much for
these kindly supporters of a divinity whom they outrage;
scandal, debauchery, seduction, that is their way of life,
and we, who are deceived by their false virtue, we stupidly
dare to revere them still.'

Clervil was very angry at this outburst but succeeded all
the same in concealing his agitation; he withdrew com-
posedly through the crowd that surrounded him.

'May Heaven,' he said calmly, 'preserve this unfortunate

girl ... may it improve her if possible, and may nobody in her house attack virtue more than I do ... I came much less to destroy it than to revive it in her heart.'

This was the result that Madame de Farneille and her daughter obtained from negotiations of which they had hoped so much. They were far from realising the deterioration that crime occasions in the minds of villains; things that would improve others make them worse, and it is in the very lessons of wisdom that they find incitement to evil.

From this moment antagonism became more intense all round; Franval and Eugénie saw clearly that they had to convince Madame de Franval of her alleged wrongdoings in a way that no longer allowed her any doubt; and Madame de Farneille, in conjunction with her daughter, planned very seriously to have Eugénie abducted. They mentioned it to Clervil, but this honest friend refused to take part in such violent deeds; he had, he said, been too ill-used in this matter to be capable of anything beyond imploring that the guilty parties be forgiven, he asked for this insistently, and constantly refused any other kind of service or mediation. What sublime feelings! Why is such nobility so rare in individuals of this calling? Or why did this unique man suffer so much? Let us begin with the attempts made by Franval.

Valmont reappeared.

'You're a fool,' Eugénie's guilty lover told him, 'you do not deserve to be my pupil; and I will thrash you before the eyes of all Paris if, at a second meeting, you do not conduct yourself more satisfactorily with my wife; you must take her, my friend, but really take her, my own eyes must convince me of her defeat ... in other words I must remove from this detestable creature all means of excuse and defence.'

'But what if she resists?' replied Valmont.

'You will use violence ... I shall take care to remove everyone. ... Frighten her, threaten her, what does it matter? I shall regard all the means of your triumph as so many services rendered by you.'

'Listen,' said Valmont then, 'I agree to your suggestion

and I give you my word that your wife will yield, but I demand one condition, I shall do nothing if you refuse it; jealousy must not enter into our arrangements, as you know; I demand therefore that you allow me to spend one quarter of an hour with Eugénie . . . you cannot imagine how I shall behave when I have enjoyed the pleasure of being with your daughter for a moment. . . .'

'But Valmont . . .'

'I understand your fears; but if you believe me to be your friend, I don't forgive them; I aspire only to the delights of seeing Eugénie alone and conversing with her for a moment.'

'Valmont,' said Franval, slightly surprised, 'you are putting much too high a price on your services; I know, like you, all the absurdities of jealousy, but I worship the girl of whom you speak and I would rather give up my fortune than her favours.'

'I do not aspire to them, keep calm.'

Franval could see clearly that among his acquintances there was no one capable of serving him like Valmont, and he was most anxious that he should not slip through his fingers.

'Well,' he told him, somewhat angrily. 'I repeat that your services are costly; in performing them like this you will regard me as having shown some recognition of them.'

'Oh, recognition is the price only of honourable services; you will never feel it for those I am going to perform for you: better still, they will make us quarrel before two months are out. . . . Come my friend, I know how a man is made . . . his failings . . . his faults . . . and all the consequences they bring; place this creature, the most evil of all, in any situation you like, and I shall not fail to predict a single result from the data you gave me. I want to be paid in advance therefore, or I shall do nothing.'

'I accept,' said Franval.

'Well,' replied Valmont, 'everything depends now on your wishes, I shall act when you want me to.'

'I need a few days for my preparations,' said Franval 'but in four at the most I am yours.'

Monsieur de Franval had brought up his daughter in such a way as to be quite sure that no excess of modesty would make her refuse to take part in the plans arranged with his friend; but he was jealous, Eugénie knew; she adored him at least as much as she was cherished by him, and she admitted to Franval, as soon as she knew what was involved, that she was very much afraid there would be some consequences to this tête-à-tête. Franval, who thought he knew Valmont well enough to be sure that there was only some intellectual pleasure for him in all this, but no danger to his heart, allayed his daughter's fears as best he could and all the preparations were made.

It was at this moment that Franval learned through servants in his mother-in-law's house who were completely in his pay that Eugénie was in great danger and Madame de Farneille was about to obtain an order to have her removed. Franval had no doubt that the plot was the work of Clervil; abandoning Valmont's plans for the moment he concerned himself only with getting rid of the unfortunate ecclesiastic whom he believed so wrongly to be the instigator of everything; he scattered money about, that powerful weapon of all vice was placed by him in many different hands: and finally six faithful villains agreed to carry out his orders.

One evening when Clervil, who often took supper at Madame de Farneille's house, was leaving alone, and on foot, he was surrounded and seized . . . he was told that this was being done on behalf of the government. He was shown a forged order, then thrown into a post-chaise and conducted in all haste to the dungeons of an isolated castle owned by Franval in the depths of the Ardennes. The unfortunate man was handed over to the concierge of this place like a criminal who had tried to take his master's life; and the greatest precautions were taken to prevent this unhappy victim, whose only wrong was to have been too indulgent towards those who had outraged him so cruelly, from ever seeing the light of day again.

Madame de Farneille was in despair. She had no doubt that her son-in-law was responsible for this deed; the effort necessary for finding Clervil again slowed down slightly the preparations for Eugénie's abduction; possessing few acquaintances and little credit it was difficult to deal with two such important objectives at the same time, but this violent action by Franval had made it necessary. They thought only of the director therefore, but all search was in vain; our villain had laid his plans so well that it was impossible to discover anything: Madame de Franval dared not question her husband too much, they had not yet spoken to each other since the last scene, but great self-interest destroys all consideration; at last she found the courage to ask her tyrannical husband if he intended, in addition to all the evil designs he had on her, to deprive her mother of the best friend she had in the world. The monster defended himself; he took hypocrisy to the extent of offering to carry out a search himself; seeing that in order to prepare the scene for Valmont, he needed to soften his wife's heart by renewing his promise to do everything to find Clervil, he lavished caresses on this credulous wife, assuring her that however unfaithful he was to her it was becoming impossible for him not to adore her in the depths of his heart; and Madame de Franval, who was always accommodating and sweet-natured, always pleased by the things that brought her close to the man who was dearer to her than life, complied with all the wishes of this faithless husband, anticipated, satisfied and shared them all, without daring to take advantage of the moment, as she should have done, in order to obtain at least better behaviour from him, which would not plunge his unhappy wife every day into an abyss of torment and woe. But if she had tried, would her attempts have been successful? Would Franval, who was so deceitful in every action of his life have been more sincere in that which, according to him, was only attractive for the sake of its material advantages? No doubt he would have promised everything for the sole pleasure of breaking all his promises, perhaps he would even have wanted people to demand oaths from him, in order to add the attractions of perjury to his horrible enjoyment.

Franval, who was now absolutely at ease, thought only of upsetting others; he behaved in his vindictive, unruly, impetuous way when he was disturbed; he desired his own tranquillity again at any price, and in order to obtain it he clumsily adopted the only means most likely to make him lose it once again. If he obtained it he used all his moral and physical facilties only to do harm to others; he was therefore always in a state of agitation, he had either to anticipate the wiles which he forced others to employ against him, or else he had to use them against others.

Everything was arranged to satisfy Valmont; and his tête-à-tête lasted nearly an hour in Eugénie's very apartment.

There, in a decorated room, Eugénie, on a pedestal, represented a young savage exhausted from the chase, leaning against the trunk of a palm tree, the branches of which concealed an infinite number of lights arranged in such a way that they illuminated the charms of this beautiful girl, emphasising them with the greatest art. The kind of little theatre where stood this animated statue was surrounded with a canal, six feet wide and filled with water which acted as a barrier to the young savage and prevented her from being approached from any side. At the edge of this encircling moat was placed Valmont's armchair, to which was attached a silken cord. By operating this thread he could turn the pedestal in such a way that he could see the object of his adoration from all sides, and her pose was such that in which ever way she was turned she looked always pleasing. Franval, hidden behind a leafy decoration, could watch simultaneously both his mistress and his friend, and the scrutiny as arranged at the last meeting was to last for half an hour. . . . Valmont took his place . . . he was intoxicated; never, he said, had so many charms appeared before his eyes. He gave way to the transports which aroused him, the cord moved unceasingly to offer him new attractions at every moment. He did not know which one to adore, which one to prefer; everything about Eugénie was so beautiful! However, the minutes passed; they go so quickly in such circumstances. The hour struck, Valmont abandoned himself, and incense rose rapidly to

the feet of the god whose sanctuary was forbidden to him.
a gauze curtain descended, it was time to go.

'Well, are you pleased?' said Franval, rejoining his
friend.

'She's a delicious creature,' replied Valmont; 'but
Franval, take my advice, do not risk anything similar with
another man, and congratulate yourself on the feelings
which, in my heart, should guarantee you against all
dangers.'

'I am relying on that,' replied Franval, seriously, 'act
now as quickly as possible.'

'Tomorrow I shall prepare your wife . . . you realise that
a preliminary conversation is necessary . . . four days after
that you can be sure of me.'

They gave each other their word and separated.

But it was only to be expected that after such an
encounter Valmont would not want to betray Madame de
Franval, or to guarantee his friend a conquest of which he
had become only too envious. Eugénie had made such a
deep impression on him that he could not renounce her; he
was determined to have her as a wife, whatever the cost
might be. Thinking it over carefully, provided he was not
repulsed by Eugénie's intrigue with her father, he was
quite certain that his fortune was equal to that of Colunce
and he was equally justified in aspiring to the same alliance;
he imagined therefore that in presenting himself as a
husband he could not be refused and that if he acted
energetically, in order to sever Eugénie's incestuous ties,
promising the family that he would succeed in this, he
could not fail to obtain the object of his admiration . . .
after a struggle with Franval, in the hope that his own
courage and skill would allow him to emerge from it
successfully. Twenty-four hours were enough for these
reflections, and Valmont, his head full of these ideas, went
to see Madame de Franval. She had been warned; it will
be remembered that during her last interview with her
husband she had become almost reconciled, or rather,
having yielded to the insidious artifices of that faithless
man, she could no longer refuse to see Valmont. She had

however brought up the question of the letters, the statements and ideas put forward by Franval; but the latter, who no longer appeared to be concerned about anything, had assured her forcefully that the most certain way of giving the impression that everything was false or no longer existed, was to see her friend as usual; if she refused to do so, he stated, she would be justifying his suspicions; the best proof that a woman can furnish of her honour, he had told her, was to continue seeing in public the man who had been mentioned in connection with her: all this was fallacious, Madame de Franval was very well aware of it, but she was hoping for an explanation from Valmont; her desire to have it, coupled with her anxiety not to displease her husband, had caused her to forget everything that should from a rational point of view have prevented her from seeing this young man. He arrived therefore and Franval hastily went out, leaving them together as on the the last occasion: the explanations would be animated and lengthy; Valmont, who was full of his ideas, cut everything short and came to the point.

'Oh, madame,' he hastened to say, 'no longer regard me as the same man who so covered himself with guilt in your eyes the last time he spoke to you; at that time I was the accomplice of your husband's wrongdoings, today I come to make them good; but have confidence in me now, madame; I beg you accept my word of honour that I do not come here to lie to you nor to impose on you in any way.'

He then admitted the story of the forged notes and letters and begged to be forgiven for having lent himself to it, he warned Madame de Franval of the new horrors that were now being demanded of him, and in order to prove his frankness he admitted his feelings for Eugénie, divulging what had taken place, and undertook to put an end to everything, to abduct Eugénie from Franval and take her to Picardy, to one of the properties owned by Madame de Farneille, if both ladies would give him permission to do so, and promise him as a reward that he could marry the girl whom he was rescuing from perdition.

Valmont's confessions seemed so truthful that Madame

de Franval could not help being convinced; Valmont was an excellent match for her daughter; after Eugénie's bad behaviour, could she expect so much? Valmont took responsibility for everything, there was no other means of ending the horrible and criminal way of life which was the despair of Madame de Franval; should she not hope moreover for a change in her husband's feelings after the break-up of the one intrigue which could really have become dangerous for her and for him? These considerations decided her, she yielded, but on condition that Valmont give her his word that he would not fight a duel with her husband, that he would go abroad after having restored Eugénie to Madame de Farneille, and would remain there until Franval had become reconciled to the loss of his illicit love, and finally agreed to the marriage. Valmont undertook everything; Madame de Franval, on her side, answered for her mother's intentions, assured him she would not oppose the plans they were making together, and Valmont retired with renewed excuses to Madame de Franval for having been capable of acting against her in all that her dishonourable husband had demanded of him. Madame de Farneille was informed of this and left for Picardy the next day while Franval, carried away by the perpetual whirlwind of his pleasures, relying completely on Valmont, and no longer fearing Clervil, fell into the trap that had been prepared with the same ease that he so often hoped to see in others, when in his turn he wanted to ensnare them.

During the last six months or so Eugénie, who was nearly seventeen, had gone out fairly often alone, or with a few of her women companions. The day before Valmont, by arrangement with his friend, was to make an attack on Madame de Franval, Eugénie went entirely alone to see a new play at the Comédie Française and afterwards set off to join her father in a house where he had arranged to meet her, so that they could go together to the one where they were both to take supper. . . . Her carriage had barely left the Faubourg Saint-Germain when ten masked men stopped the horses, opened the door, seized Eugénie and threw her into a post-chaise, beside Valmont, who, doing all he could to stifle her cries, urged the most extreme haste and found himself out of Paris in no time.

It had unfortunately been impossible to get rid of Eugénie's servants and her carriage, which meant that Franval was informed very quickly. Valmont had counted on Franval's uncertainty about the direction he had taken, and on the two or three hours' start that he would have. It was only necessary for him to reach Madame de Farneille's property, for there two reliable women and a post-chaise would be waiting to take Eugénie to the frontier and to a hiding-place unknown even to Valmont, who was to go at once to Holland and would reappear in order to marry his mistress, as soon as Madame de Farneille and her daughter let him know that there were no more obstacles; but fate allowed these careful plans to fail, thanks to the horrible designs of the villain concerned.

When Franval was informed he lost not a moment, he went to the posting station and asked for what routes horses had been hired since six o'clock in the evening. At seven o'clock a closed carriage had left for Lyons and at eight a coach had gone to Picardy; Franval did not hesitate, the Lyons carriage was certainly not interesting from his point of view, but a coach on the way towards a province where Madame de Farneille owned land . . . that must be it, it would be madness to doubt it; he immediately there-fore had the posting station's eight best horses harnessed to the carriage in which he was travelling, he made his servants take nags, he bought and loaded pistols while the horses were being harnessed and flew with the speed of an arrow where love, despair and vengeance led him. While changing horses at Senlis he learnt that the coach he was pursuing had only just left. . . . Franval ordered light-ning speed; to his misfortune, he overtook the coach: his servants and he, pistols in hand, stopped Valmont's postilion, and the impetuous Franval, recognising his adversary, blew his brains out before he could defend himself, tore Eugénie out of the coach in a state of collapse, leapt with her into his own and was back in Paris before ten in the morning. Barely concerned about all that had happened Franval paid attention only to Eugénie. . . . Had not the treacherous Valmont tried to take advantage of circumstances? Was Eugénie still faithful to him, and had his guilty alliance not been besmirched? Mademoiselle de Franval reassured her father. Valmont had done no more than outline his plan to her and, full of hope that he would soon marry her, he had refrained from desecrating the shrine before which he wanted to offer unsullied homage; Eugénie's assurances satisfied Franval. . . . But his wife . . . was she aware of these moves? Had she been a party to them? Eugénie, who had had time to find out, assured him that everything was the work of her mother, whom she called by a vast number of hateful names, and that this fatal meeting, at which Franval had imagined that Valmont was preparing to serve him so well, was definitely the one at which he had betrayed him in the most shameless fashion.

'Ah,' said Franval in a fury, 'why has he not a thousand lives . . . I would wrest them all from him, one after the other . . . And my wife! . . . when I tried to appease her . . . she was the first to deceive me . . . the creature who is thought to be so gentle . . . that angel of virtue! Ah, traitress, traitress, you will pay dearly for your crime . . . my vengeance has need of blood, and if necessary I shall go and draw it with my own lips from your perfidious veins. . . . Calm yourself, Eugénie,' continued Franval, in violent mood, 'yes, calm yourself, you need rest, go and enjoy some for a few hours, I will deal with all this alone.'

However, Madame de Farneille had posted spies all along the road and was soon informed of all that had taken place; knowing that her granddaughter had been brought back and Valmont killed, she went at once to Paris. In a fury she summoned her advisers together; she was told that Valmont's murder would deliver Franval into her hands, that his credit, of which she was afraid, would vanish instantly, and that she would immediately assume control again both of her daughter and of Eugénie; but she was advised to avoid publicity, and in case she incurred destructive legal action, to seek an order which could put her son-in-law under restraint. Franval was informed at once of this advice and of the ensuing consequences; learning simultaneously that the affair was becoming public knowledge, and that his mother-in-law was awaiting his undoing only in order to take advantage of it, he sped at once to Versailles, saw the minister, told him everything and was merely advised in return to go and hide at once in the property he owned in Alsace, on the Swiss border. Franval immediately went back home and, determined to succeed in his revenge, to punish his wife's treachery and to find himself still in possession of things dear enough to Madame de Farneille for her not to dare, at least from a political point of view, to take action against him, he decided that he would only leave for Valmor, the property where the minister had advised him to go, in the company of his wife and daughter. . . . But would Madame de Franval agree to this? Feeling herself guilty of the kind of treachery which had led to all these events, would she be able to go so far away? Would she dare to entrust herself without fear to the protection of an outraged husband? Franval was anxious about all this; in order to discover how far he could go, he immediately went to his wife's apartment. She had already been informed of everything.

'Madame,' he said coldly, 'through your hasty indiscretion you have plunged me into an abyss of misfortunes; while I criticise the results I nevertheless approve the cause, which is no doubt your love for your daughter and for me; and since the first wrongs were committed by me, I ought to forget those that followed. Dear and loving half of my life,' he went on, falling at his wife's feet, 'will you accept a reconciliation that nothing in the future can impair? I have come to offer it to you, and this is my pledge. . . .'

He then placed at his wife's feet all the forged papers which had been alleged to be the correspondence with Valmont.

'Burn it all, my dear friend, I beg you,' the traitor continued, with feigned tears, 'and forgive what jealousy made me do: let us banish all bitterness between us; I was very much in the wrong, I confess; but who knows if

Valmont, in order to succeed in his designs, did not incriminate me in your eyes more than I deserve . . . If he had dared to say that I could have ceased to love you . . . that you had not always been the most precious and most estimable creature in the world for me; ah, dear angel, if he had disgraced himself with these calumnies, what a good thing I did in depriving the world of such a trickster and impostor!'

'Oh, sir,' said Madame de Franval, in tears, 'is it possible to conceive the atrocities that you committed against me? How can you expect me to have any confidence in you after such horrors?'

'I want you to love me still, oh most loving and lovable of wives! Accuse only my mind of my many faults, but be convinced that my heart, over which you always reigned, could never be capable of betraying you . . . yes, I want you to know that every single mistake of mine has brought me truly closer to you. . . . The further I moved away from my dear wife, the less I could see any possibility of finding her again in anything; neither pleasures nor feelings equalled those that my inconstancy caused me to lose, and in the very arms of her image, I regretted reality. . . . Oh, beloved and divine friend, where could I find a soul like yours? Where could I find the favours that are enjoyed in your arms? Yes, I abjure all my errors . . . only to restore to your wounded heart the love so justly destroyed by wrongdoing . . . which I abjure down to the very memory.'

It was impossible for Madame de Franval to resist such loving remarks from a man whom she still adored; can one hate a person one has loved deeply? Can an attractive woman with a subtle and sensitive soul remain unmoved when she sees at her feet the man who had been so dear to her, bathed in tears? Sobs escaped her . . .

'I,' she said, clasping her husband's hands against her heart . . . 'I, who never ceased to worship you, cruel man! It is I whose heart you are wantonly breaking! Ah, Heaven is my witness, of all the scourges with which you could strike me, the fear of having lost your love, or of being suspected by you, became the most painful of all. . . . And what is more, whom did you choose in order to outrage me? My daughter! It is with her hands that you pierce my heart . . . do you want to force me to hate her whom nature has made so dear to me?'

'Ah,' said Franval, still more ardently, 'I want to restore her to your love, I want her to abjure, on her knees, like me, both her shamelessness and her wrongdoings . . . may she be forgiven, like me. Let the three of us think only of our mutual happiness. I will give you back your daughter . . . give me back my wife . . . and let us flee.'

'Flee, gracious heaven!'

'My escapade is being talked about. . . . I could be ruined tomorrow. . . . My friends, the minister, everyone has advised me to make a journey to Valmor . . . will you deign to follow me there, my love? At the moment when I kneel to ask forgiveness would you break my heart by refusing?'

'You frighten me. . . . This business . . .'

'Is regarded as a murder, and not as a duel.'

'Oh, heavens! And I am the cause of it! Give your orders: do as you wish with me, beloved husband. . . . I will follow you if necessary to the ends of the earth. . . . Oh, I am the most wretched of women!'

'Say instead the most fortunate, certainly, since every moment of my life will be devoted in future to transforming into flowers the thorns I strew beneath your feet . . . is a desert not enough when one is in love? Besides, this will not last for ever; my friends have been informed and will take action.'

'And my mother . . . I would like to see her. . . .'

'Ah, take good care not to, dear friend, I have certain proofs that she is inciting Valmont's parents . . . that she herself, along with them, is seeking my downfall. . . .'

'She is incapable of doing so; cease to imagine these treacherous horrors; her soul is made for loving and has never known deceit . . . you never appreciated her fully, Franval . . . why were you not able to love her as I did! With her we would have found happiness on earth! She was the angel of peace offered by heaven to mend the errors of your ways, your injustice repulsed her love, which was always prepared to accept your affection, and through indiscretion or capriciousness, through ingratitude or licentiousness, you voluntarily deprived yourself of the best and most affectionate friend that nature had created for you: shall I not see her then?'

'No, I earnestly ask you not to . . . moments are so precious! You will write to her, you will describe my repentance to her . . . perhaps she will yield to my remorse . . . perhaps I will one day regain her esteem and her love; everything will settle down, we shall return . . . we shall return to enjoy in her arms her forgiveness and her affection. . . . But let us go away now, my dear . . . we must do so within an hour, and the carriages await us.'

Madame de Franval was frightened and no longer dared to make any reply; she prepared to leave: Franval's wishes were her commands. The traitor sped to his daughter; he took her to her mother's feet; the deceitful creature threw herself on her knees before her just as treacherously as her father had done: she wept, begged her forgiveness and obtained it. Madame de Franval embraced her; it is so difficult to forget that one is a mother, however much one's children have harmed one . . . the voice of nature is so commanding in a sensitive soul that one single tear from these sacred creatures is enough to make us forget twenty years of errors or wrongs on their side.

They left for Valmor. The extreme haste with which they were obliged to make their journey justified, in the eyes of Madame de Franval, who was always credulous and blind, the small number of servants they took with them. Crime avoids the eyes of others . . . it fears them all; since there can be safety only in secrecy, criminals shroud themselves in mystery when they want to act.

In the country all promises were kept; constant attention, consideration, respect and marks of tenderness on one side . . . the most violent love on the other, all this lavishness seduced the unfortunate Madame de Franval. . . . Far from everywhere, separated from her mother, living in the depths of a terrible solitude, she was happy because she had, she said, her husband's love and because her daughter, who was constantly beside her, busied herself only with pleasing her.

The apartments of Eugénie and her father were no longer adjacent to each other; Franval lodged at the far end of the château and Eugénie close to her mother; and at Valmor decorum, good behaviour and modesty replaced to an outstanding extent all the licentiousness of the capital. Every night Franval went to his wife, and in the midst of innocence, naïveté and love the rascal dared to nourish hope by his vile conduct. This villain was cruel enough not to be disarmed by the ardent caresses bestowed on him freely by the most sensitive of wives, and it was from the very torch of love that he lit that of revenge.

It can be imagined however that Franval's assiduous attraction to Eugénie did not slacken. In the morning, while her mother's toilet was being performed, Eugénie would meet her father in a remote part of the gardens, obtaining from him in her turn both the necessary information on how to conduct herself from day to day and also the favours that she was far from wishing to relinquish completely to her rival.

They had only been in this retreat for a week when Franval learned that Valmont's family were taking all possible action against him, and that the matter was going to be treated with extreme seriousness; it was becoming impossible, apparently, to pass it off as a duel, there had unfortunately been too many witnesses; in addition, Franval was also told, Madame de Farneille was certainly at the head of her son-in-law's enemies, intending to complete his downfall by depriving him of his liberty, or by forcing him to leave France, so that she could restore to her side the two cherished beings who were separated from her.

Franval showed these letters to his wife; she at once took up her pen in order to calm her mother, to make her think differently and to describe to her the happiness she had been enjoying since misfortune had softened the heart of her unhappy husband; she assured her mother moreover that it would be vain to persuade her to return to Paris with her daughter, that she was determined not to leave Valmor until her husband's affairs were settled; and that if the wickedness of his enemies or the absurdities of his judges made him liable to a sentence which would ruin his reputation, she was quite determined to leave France with him.

Franval thanked his wife; but since he had no desire to await whatever lay in store for him, he warned her that he was going to spend some time in Switzerland, that he would leave Eugénie with her, and entreated them both not to leave Valmor until his future was settled; that whatever happened he would return to spend twenty-four hours with his dear wife in order to decide together on the means of returning to Paris, if nothing prevented this, or otherwise to go and live somewhere in safety.

When these decisions had been taken Franval, who had not forgotten that his wife's imprudence with Valmont was the one cause of his setbacks, and who thought only of revenge, told his daughter that he would wait for her on the far side of the grounds. He shut himself up with her in a remote *pavillon* and after making her swear the most unquestioning obedience to everything he was going to say, he kissed her and spoke as follows:

'You are losing me, my daughter . . . perhaps for ever. . . .'

Eugénie burst into tears.

'Calm yourself, my angel,' he told her, 'the recovery of our happiness rests entirely with you, and in France, or elsewhere, we can once more be as happy, or almost so, as we were before. I hope, Eugénie, that you are entirely convinced that your mother is the sole cause of all our misfortunes, you know that I have not lost sight of revenge; if I have hidden this from my wife, you have known the reasons for it, you have approved of them, you have helped me with this prudent concealment; we have reached the end now, Eugénie; we must act; your peace of mind depends on it, and what you are going to undertake ensures mine for ever; you understand me, I hope, and you are too intelligent to be alarmed for one moment by what I am suggesting to you. . . . Yes, my daughter, we must act, we must do so at once, we must do so without remorse, and you must perform the deed. Your mother tried to make you unhappy, she has tarnished the love she demands, she has lost her rights to it; from that time onwards she is no more to you than an ordinary woman, but she has even become your most deadly enemy; now, the law of nature that is most deeply engraved in our hearts is that we should rid ourselves first, if we can, of those who conspire against us; this sacred law, which continually directs and inspires us, does not make us love other people in preference to what we owe to ourselves. . . . Ourselves first, others next, that is the law of nature; as a result, no respect, no consideration for others when they prove that our unhappiness or our downfall is the one thing they desire; to behave differently, my daughter, would be to prefer others to ourselves, and that would be absurd. Now let us come to the motives which must determine the action I am advising you to take.

'I am forced to go away, you know why; if I leave you with this woman, she will be won over by her mother and within a month she will take you back to Paris; since the recent scandal will prevent you from being married you can be very sure that these two cruel women will only achieve authority over you in order to put you in a convent where you will weep for ever over your weakness and the delights we have lost. It is your grandmother, Eugénie, who is taking action against me, it is she who is joining forces with my enemies to complete my downfall; can such actions on her part have any other aim except that of winning you back, and will she take you without locking you up? The more my position deteriorates, the more power and credit are assumed by our tormentors. Now, we must not doubt that your mother is secretly at the head of this faction, we must not doubt that she will join them again as soon as I go away; yet they only desire to ruin me in order to make you the most unfortunate of women; we must therefore weaken them without delay, and their greatest source of energy will be removed with the disappearance of Madame de Franval. If we act differently and I take you away with me your mother will be angry and will rejoin her mother at once; from that moment, Eugénie, there will be no peace for us; we shall be sought out and pursued everywhere, not one country will have the right to give us a resting-place, not one refuge on the face of the earth will become sacred or inviolable in the eyes of the monsters whose rage will pursue us; are you unaware how far these hateful weapons of despotism and tyranny can reach, when they are paid for in gold and directed by evil? If your mother is dead, on the contrary, Madame de Farneille, who loves her more than she does you, and who takes part in everything for her sake, seeing her faction deprived of the only being who truly links her to it, will abandon everything and will no longer incite my enemies or rouse them against me. After that one of two alternatives will prevail: either the Valmont affair will be settled, and nothing will prevent our return to Paris any longer; or else it will go against me and we shall be forced to go abroad but we shall at least be sheltered from the attacks of the Farneille, who, as long as your mother is alive, will only aim at bringing about our misfortune because, once again, she believes that her daughter's happiness can only be achieved through our downfall.

'From whatever angle you look at our situation therefore you will see that Madame de Franval disturbs our peace of mind, and her detestable existence is the most certain obstacle to our happiness.

'Eugénie, Eugénie,' Franval went on with warmth, taking both his daughter's hands in his . . . 'dear Eugénie, you love me, do you want therefore, through fear of a deed so essential to our interests, to lose for ever the man who adores you? Oh dear and beloved Eugénie, take your decision, you can keep only one of your parents; you are forced to be a parricide, now you can choose only the heart which your criminal dagger will pierce; either your mother must perish, or you must renounce me . . . what am I saying, you will have to kill me yourself. . . . Alas, could I live without you? . . . do you think it is possible for me to exist without my Eugénie? Could I resist the memory of the pleasures I have enjoyed in your arms . . . these delightful pleasnres lost to my senses for ever? Your crime, Eugénie, your crime is the same in both cases; either you destroy a mother who hates you, and who lives only to cause your misfortune, or you must assassinate a father who exists only for you. Choose, choose therefore, Eugénie, and if it is I whom you condemn, do not hesitate, ungrateful girl, pierce without pity this heart whose only error was to love you too much, I shall bless the blows which come from your hand and my last sigh will be to adore you.'

Franval became silent in order to hear his daughter's reply; but deep thought seemed to make her hesitate . . . at last she rushed into her father's arms.

'Oh you whom I shall love all my life,' she cried, 'can you doubt my decision? Can you suspect I lack courage? Put a weapon into my hands at once, and she who is proscribed by her own horrible deeds and the need for your safety shall soon fall beneath my blows; instruct me, Franval, tell me what to do, go, since this is essential for your peace of mind . . . I will act during your absence, I will inform you of everything; but whatever happens . . . as soon as our enemy is destroyed, do not leave me alone in this château, I insist . . . come and take me away, or tell me where I may join you.'

'Beloved daughter,' said Franval, embracing the monster whom he had seduced only too well, 'I knew I should find in you all the feelings of love and determination necessary to our mutual happiness. . . . Take this box . . . death is contained within it. . . .'

Eugénie took the fatal box and renewed her pledges to her father; the other decisions were made; it was arranged that she would wait for the outcome of the lawsuit, and that the projected crime would either take place or not, depending on what would be decided for or against her father. They separated, Franval rejoined his wife, he took audacity and hypocrisy to the point of weeping bitterly in front of her until he received, without fail, the touching and innocent caresses of this celestial angel. Then, when it had been agreed that she would definitely remain in Alsace with her daughter, whatever the outcome of the legal action, the villain mounted his horse and rode away, away from the innocence and virtue which had been so long besmirched by his crimes.

Franval went to settle in Basle, in order to be safe from the judicial action which could be taken against him and at the same time remain as near as possible to Valmor, so that failing his presence, his letters could maintain Eugénie in the frame of mind he wanted. It was about twenty-five leagues from Basle to Valmor, but communications were easy enough, although they passed through the midst of the Black Forest, for him to have news of his daughter once a week. In case of emergency Franval had taken vast sums of money with him, but more in notes than in silver. Let us leave him to establish himself in Switzerland and return to his wife.

Nothing could be as pure and sincere as the intentions of this remarkable woman; she had promised her husband to remain in this country estate until he gave her fresh orders; nothing would have made her change her mind, she assured Eugénie of this every day. . . . Unfortunately Eugénie was too remote in an unfortunate way to have the confidence that this honourable mother was fitted to inspire in her; she still shared Franval's unjust attitude—a feeling that he kept alive in his letters—and imagined that she could have no greater enemy in the world than her mother. There was nothing however that the latter did not do in order to remove from her daughter the invincible remoteness that this ungrateful girl preserved in the depths of her heart; her mother overwhelmed her with caresses and love, she looked forward affectionately with her to her husband's safe return, taking gentleness and compliments to the point of sometimes thanking Eugénie and allowing her all the merit for this happy conversion; then she was heartbroken at having become the innocent cause of the new misfortunes which threatened Franval; far from accusing Eugénie, she blamed only herself, and, pressing her against her bosom, she asked her with tears if she could ever forgive her. . . . The atrocious Eugénie resisted these angelic remarks, this perverse heart no longer heard the voice of nature, vice had barred all the ways that might have led to it. . . . Withdrawing coldly from her mother's arms, she looked at her with eyes that were sometimes wild, and thought, in order to give herself courage: *How false this woman is . . . how treacherous she is . . . she embraced me the same way on the day she had me kidnapped.* But these unjust reproaches were only the abominable sophistries with which criminals bolster themselves up, when they want to silence the voice of duty. When she had Eugénie kidnapped, for the sake of her daughter's happiness and her own peace of mind, and in the interests of virtue, Madame de Franval had been able to conceal her actions; such pretences are only disapproved of by the guilty person whom they deceive, they do not offend the virtuous. Eugénie resisted all Madame de Franval's affection because she wanted to commit a horrible deed, and by no means because of the wrongs of a mother who certainly committed none against her daughter.

Near the end of the first month at Valmor, Madame de Farneille wrote to her daughter that the lawsuit against her husband was becoming extremely serious, and that since there was a danger that he would be condemned, the return of Madame de Franval and Eugénie was becoming vitally necessary, just as much to impress the public, who were saying the worst possible things, as for joining with her in soliciting some arrangement which could disarm justice and deal with the guilty party without sentencing him to death.

Madame de Franval, who had decided to keep no secrets from her daughter, immediately showed her this letter; Eugénie looked hard at her mother and coldly asked her, now that she had received this sad news, what attitude she wanted to take?

'I do not know,' replied Madame de Franval, 'In fact, what purpose do we serve here? Would we not be a thousand times more useful to my husband if we took the advice of my mother?'

'You are in charge, madame,' replied Eugénie, 'I am there to do as you say, and I will certainly obey you.'

But Madame de Franval, realising clearly from her

daughter's dry tones that this decision did not please her, said that she would continue to wait, that she would write again, and that Eugénie could be sure that if she failed to carry out Franval's intentions, it would only be in the certainty of being more useful to him in Paris than at Valmor.

Another month passed in this way, during which Franval did not cease to write to his wife and daughter, and to receive from them the kind of letters most likely to please him, since he saw only in those from the former a perfect obedience to his wishes and in those from the latter the most complete determination to carry out the projected crime, as soon as events demanded it, or as soon as Madame de Franval appeared to yield to the demands of her mother; 'for,' said Eugénie in her letters, 'if I see nothing in your wife except uprightness and honesty, and if the friends who are looking after your interests in Paris succeed in settling matters satisfactorily, I will hand back to you the task you entrusted to me, and you will carry it out yourself when we are together, if you deem it to be a suitable moment, unless, however, you order me to act in any case and you find it indispensable, then I will assume full responsibility, you may be sure of that.'

Franval gave his approval in his reply to all that his daughter told him, and such was the last letter that he received from her and the last that he wrote. The following post brought none; Franval became anxious; he received just as little satisfaction from the next post, he became desperate, and since his natural agitation no longer allowed him to wait, he immediately formed the plan of going to Valmor himself to know the cause of the delays which tormented him so cruelly.

He mounted his horse, followed by a faithful valet; he was to arrive two days later, too late at night to be recognised by anyone; at the entrance to the woods which surrounded the Château de Valmor, merging with the Black Forest towards the east, six well-armed men stopped Franval and his lackey; they demanded his purse; these rascals were well informed, they knew to whom they were speaking, they knew that Franval, who was in trouble, never moved without his wallet and a vast amount of gold. . . . The valet showed resistance, and was stretched out lifeless beside his horse; Franval, sword in hand, dismounted, rushed upon these unfortunates, wounded three of them and found himself surrounded by the others; they took from him all he had, and although they did not succeed in wresting his weapon from him, the robbers escaped as soon as they had stripped him; Franval followed them, but the brigands went like the wind with their booty and the horses, and it became impossible to know which direction they had taken.

It was a horrible night, with a north wind and hail . . . all the elements seemed to have been let loose against this wretched man. . . . There are perhaps cases in which nature is revolted by the crimes of the man she pursues and wishes to overwhelm him, before taking him back to her, with all the scourges in her power. . . . Franval, half naked, but still holding his sword, left this fatal spot as best he could and went towards Valmor. He was not well acquainted with the surroundings of a property which he knew only from his recent stay there, he lost his way among the obscure paths of this forest which was entirely unknown to him. . . . Exhausted by fatigue and pain . . . devoured by anxiety, tormented by the storm, he threw himself to the ground and there, the first tears he had shed in his life came flooding to his eyes. . . .

'Wretched that I am,' he cried, 'so everything combines to crush me at last . . . to make me feel remorse . . . the hand of misfortune causes it to penetrate my soul; deceived by the pleasures of prosperity, I have always been unmindful of it. . . . Oh you, whom I outraged so grievously, you who at this moment are perhaps becoming a prey to my barbarous fury! . . . adorable wife . . . the world was made glorious by your existence, does it still hold you? Has the hand of Heaven put a stop to my horrible deeds? Eugénie! Over-credulous daughter . . . too unworthily seduced by my terrible artifices . . . has nature softened your heart? Has she ended the cruel effects of my ascendancy and your weakness? Is it time? Is it time, just heavens?'

All at once the plaintive and majestic sound of several bells, ringing out mournfully towards the clouds, added to the horror of his fate. . . . He became alarmed and frightened.

'What do I hear?' he cried, rising . . . 'Barbarous girl . . . is it death? Is it revenge? Are these the furies of hell coming to complete their work? What do these sounds tell me? Where am I? Do I hear them? Oh Heaven, complete your punishment of my guilt. . . .'

'Great God,' he cried, prostrating himself, 'suffer me to mingle my voice with those who implore you at this moment . . . see my remorse and Thy power, forgive me for having neglected Thee . . . and deign to grant the wishes . . . the first wishes I dare to bring to Thee! Supreme Being . . . preserve virtue, preserve her who was the finest image of Thee in this world; may these sounds, alas, these melancholy sounds be not those that I fear.'

And Franval, who was lost, no longer knowing either what he did or where he was going, uttering only disjointed words, followed the path before him. Then he heard someone, he came to himself, he listened . . . it was a man on horseback. . . .

'Whoever you are,' cried Franval, going towards him . . . 'whoever you may be, have pity on an unfortunate man whom sorrow leads astray . . . I am ready to kill myself . . . tell me, help me, if you are a man and one who feels sympathy . . . deign to save me from myself.'

'Heavens!' replied a voice too well known to the unhappy Franval, 'what, you here! . . . Oh Heavens, away with you!'

And Clervil . . . it was he, it was this worthy mortal who had escaped from Franval's bonds, whom fate was sending towards this unfortunate man, at the saddest moment of his life . . . Clervil leapt off his horse and fell into the arms of his enemy.

'Is it you, sir?' asked Franval, pressing this honest man to his bosom, 'is it you, before whom I should reproach myself for so many horrible deeds?'

'Calm yourself, sir, calm yourself; I am thrusting from me the misfortunes which have recently surrounded me, I no longer remember those which you brought me, when Heaven allows me to be useful to you . . . and I shall be so, sir, in a cruel fashion, no doubt, but a necessary one. . . . Let us be seated . . . let us cast ourselves at the foot of this cypress, only its sorrowful leaves can make you a fitting crown now. . . . O my dear Franval, what setbacks I have to recount to you! Weep, oh my friend, tears bring relief to you, and I must wring much more bitter ones from your eyes yet. . . . The days of delight have passed . . . they have vanished for you like a dream, only the days of sorrow remain to you.'

'Oh, sir, I understand you . . . these bells . . .'

'They will carry to the feet of the Supreme Being . . . the homage and vows of the sorrowing inhabitants of Valmor, whom the Eternal only allows to know an angel in order to pity and regret her. . . .'

Franval turned the tip of his sword towards his heart and was about to end his days. But Clervil prevented this furious deed.

'No, no, my friend,' he cried, 'you must not die, but make good your faults. Listen to me, I have much to tell you, calm is needed to hear them.'

'Well, sir, speak, I am listening to you; bury the dagger slowly in my breast, it is fitting that I should be tormented in the same way as I tried to treat others.'

'I shall be brief concerning myself, sir,' said Clervil. 'After a few months of the horrible imprisonment into which you plunged me, I was fortunate enough to influence my jailer; he opened the doors for me; I commended him to conceal with the greatest care the injustice that you had allowed yourself to do me. He will not speak of it, dear Franval, never will he speak of it.'

'Oh, sir . . .'

'Listen to me, I repeat, I have many other things to tell you. Once back in Paris I learnt of your unfortunate escapade . . . your departure . . . I shared the tears of Madame de Farneille . . . they were even more sincere than you believed; I joined with this worthy woman in pressing Madame de Franval to restore Eugénie to us, their presence being more necessary in Paris than in Alsace. . . . You had forbidden her to abandon Valmor . . . she obeyed you . . . she sent us these orders, she told us of her unwillingness to disobey them; she hesitated as long as she could . . . you were condemned to death, Franval, you stand condemned now. You are to lose your head, as though guilty of highway robbery: neither the solicitations of Madame de Farneille nor the endeavours of your relatives and friends were able to sway the sword of justice; you have succumbed, you are destroyed for ever . . . you are ruined . . . all your possessions have been seized. . . .' Franval started in fury a second time. 'Listen to me, sir, listen to me, I demand it of you as reparation for your crimes, I demand it in the name of Heaven which your repentance can still disarm. At this moment we wrote to Madame de Franval, we told her everything: her mother informed her that her presence having become indispensable, she was sending me to Valmor in order to make her decide definitely on departure: I followed the letter; but unfortunately it arrived before I did; it was too late when I arrived . . . your horrible plot had been only too successful; I found Madame de Franval dying. . . . Oh, sir, what a villainous woman! But your state touches me, I cease to reproach you for your crimes. Hear all. Eugénie could not tolerate this sight: her repentance, when I arrived, was already evident in tears and the most bitter sobs. . . . Oh, sir, how can I describe to you the cruel effect of these diverse situations. . . . Your wife dying . . . disfigured by convulsions and pain . . . Eugénie, restored to natural feeling, uttering terrible cries, admitting herself to be guilty, invoking death, wanting to kill herself in turn at the feet of those whom she was imploring and clinging to her mother's bosom, trying to revive with her breath, to warm her with her tears, to move her with her remorse; such, sir, were the terrible sights which met my eyes when I entered your apartment, Madame de Franval recognised me . . . she grasped my hands . . . wetting them with her tears, and pronounced a few words that I heard with difficulty, they could barely be heard for the palpitations caused by the poison . . . she made excuses for you . . . she implored Heaven on your behalf . . . above all she asked for pardon on her daughter's behalf. . . . You see, barbarous man, the last thoughts, the last vows of her whom you were rending asunder were still for your happiness. I gave her all my care; I urged the servants to give more, I employed all the most renowned medical men . . . I multiplied consolations to your Eugénie; touched by her horrible state, I did not think I should refuse them to her; nothing succeeded; your unhappy wife breathed her last with shudders and indescribable torments . . . at this final stage, sir, I saw one of the sudden effects of remorse which had been unknown to me until that moment. Eugénie hurled herself upon her mother and died at the same time as she did: we believed that she had only fainted. . . . No, all her faculties were extinguished; her organs had been absorbed by the shock of the situation and had been annihilated at the same time, she had truly died from the violent shock of remorse, from sorrow and despair. . . . Yes, sir, both of them are lost to you; and these bells which you can still hear tolling celebrate simultaneously two creatures, both for your happiness, whom your crimes have made victims of their attachment to you, and their images, stained with blood, will pursue you to the very depths of the tomb.

'Oh, dear Franval, was I mistaken when I urged you in the past to come out of the abyss where your passions were hurling you; and will you blame and despise those who take the part of virtue? Are they wrong in fact to pay homage at its shrine when they see crime surrounded with so many troubles and scourges?'

Clervil was silent. He looked at Franval; he saw him petrified by sorrow; there was a fixed look in his eyes, tears streamed from them, but no expression could reach his lips. Clervil asked him the reason why he was nearly naked, and Franval told him briefly.

'Ah, sir,' cried this generous mortal, 'how happy I am, even in the midst of the horrors that surround me, that I can at least ease the state you are in. I was going to find you at Basle, I was going to tell you everything, I was going to offer you what little I possess. . . . Accept it, I beg you; I am not rich, you know, but here are a hundred louis . . . they are my savings, they are all I have . . . I demand from you . . .'

'Generous man,' cried Franval, embracing the knees of this honest and rare friend, 'you give them to me? Heavens, do I need anything after the losses I have suffered! And it is you . . . you whom I have treated so badly . . . it is you who fly to my help.'

'Should one remember insults when misfortune overwhelms him who can insult us? The revenge due to him in this case is to comfort him; and why overwhelm him again when his reproaches tear us asunder? . . . Sir, that is the voice of nature; you can see clearly that the sacred worship of a Supreme Being does not contradict it as you used to imagine, since the counsel inspired by one is only the sacred law of the other.'

'No,' replied Franval, rising; 'no, sir, I no longer need anything; Heaven, leaving me this last possession,' he went on, indicating his sword, 'teaches me the use I should make of it . . .' He looked at it. 'It is the same, yes, dear and unique friend, it is the same weapon that my angelic wife seized one day in order to pierce her bosom, when I was overwhelming her with horrors and calumnies . . . it is the same . . . I would perhaps find traces of her sacred blood upon it . . . my own must efface them. . . . Let us go further . . . let us find some cottages where I can acquaint you with my last wishes . . . and then we shall leave each other for ever.'

They walked on. They looked for a path which could bring them nearer to some habitation. . . . The night still shrouded the forest in darkness . . . melancholy singing was heard, the dim light of torches suddenly dispersed the darkness and cast a glow of horror which could only be conceived by sensitive souls; the sound of the bells redoubled; to these sorrowful sounds, which were still barely perceptible, was added the thunder which had remained silent until this moment, breaking out in the sky, mingling its crashes with the other funereal sounds. The lightning which furrowed the clouds, eclipsing at intervals the sinister light of the torches, seemed to dispute with the inhabitants of the earth the right to conduct to the tomb the woman accompanied by this cortège, everything inspired horror, everything breathed desolation . . . it seemed to be the eternal bereavement of nature.

'What is this?' cried Franval, with emotion.

'Nothing,' replied Clervil, seizing his friend's hand and leading him aside from the path.

'Nothing? You are deceiving me, I want to see what it is.'

He rushed forward . . . he saw a coffin:

'Gracious Heaven!' he cried, 'it is she, it is she, may God allow me to see her again. . . .'

At the request of Clervil, who saw that it was impossible to calm this unhappy man, the priests moved away in silence. . . . Distractedly Franval rushed towards the coffin, he tore from it the sad remains of the woman he had so deeply offended; he seized the body in his arms, laid it down at the foot of a tree, and hurled himself upon it with the delirium of despair.

'Oh you,' he cried, beside himself, 'you whose life was extinguished by my barbarous deeds, touching creature whom I idolise still, see your husband who dares to demand at your feet his pardon and his grace; do not imagine that I do this in order to survive you, no, no, it is so that the Eternal God, touched by your virtues, may condescend to pardon me as he does you . . . you need bloodshed, dear wife, you need it so that you may be revenged . . . you shall be. . . . Ah! see my tears first, and see my repentance; I am going to follow you, beloved shade . . . but who shall receive my murdered soul, if you do not intercede on my behalf? Rejected by God as by you, do you want me to be condemned to the terrible tortures of hell, when I repent so sincerely of my crimes? Forgive them, dear heart, and see how I avenge them.'

At these words, Franval, escaping Clervil's eye, ran the sword that he was holding twice through his body; his impure blood flowed over the victim and seemed to shrink her more than it avenged her.

'Oh my friend!' he said to Clervil, 'I am dying, but I am dying in the midst of remorse. . . . Tell those who remain to me both of my deplorable end and of my crimes, tell them that it is thus that the melancholy slave of his passions should die, he who is base enough to have stifled in his heart the cry of duty and of nature. Allow me to share the coffin of my unfortunate wife, without my remorse I should have deserved to do so, but this makes me worthy of it, and I demand it. Farewell.'

Clervil carried out the wishes of this unfortunate man, the cortège began to move forward once more; soon an eternal resting-place swallowed up for ever a husband and wife born to love each other, made for happiness, and who should have enjoyed it without remorse, if crime and its fearful disorders, beneath the guilty hand of one of them, had not changed into serpents all the roses of their life.

The honest ecclesiastic soon took back to Paris the horrible details of these various catastrophes. Nobody was upset by Franval's death, only his life had caused anger, but his wife was mourned, most bitterly so; and what creature in fact was more precious, more attractive in the eyes of mankind than the one who had only cherished, respected and cultivated the earthly virtues, to find, at every step, ill-fortune and sorrow?

THE HORSE-CHESTNUT
FLOWER

It is alleged, I would not vouch for it, but some learned men assure us that the flower of the horse-chestnut tree definitely possesses the same smell as that abundant seed which it has pleased nature to place within the loins of men for the reproduction of their kind.

A young girl of about fifteen, who had never left her father's house, was walking one day with her mother and a sophisticated Abbé down an avenue of horse-chestnut trees whose flowers filled the air with the scent which we have just taken the liberty to describe.

'Oh good gracious, mother, what an odd smell,' said the girl, not realising where it was coming from . . . 'what is it, it's a smell I know.'

'Be quiet, mademoiselle, don't make remarks of that kind, I beg you.'

'But why not, mother, I don't see what's wrong in telling you that I've smelt it before, and I definitely have.'

'But, mademoiselle . . .'

'But, mother, I recognise it, really I do; Monsieur Abbé, tell me, I beg you, what's wrong in my saying to mother that I recognise that smell?'

'Mademoiselle,' said the Abbé, adjusting his jabot and

speaking in a piping voice, 'there is certainly nothing very wrong in the fact itself; but we are walking beneath horse-chestnut trees and we botanists admit that horse-chestnut flowers . . .'

'Well, horse-chestnut flowers . . .?'

'Well, mademoiselle, they smell of spunk.'

THE CHASTISED HUSBAND

A MAN WHO WAS already middle-aged decided to get married, although he had lived without a wife until then, and in view of his inclinations the most serious mistake he probably made was to choose a young girl of eighteen, with the most attractive face in the world and a most pleasing figure. Taking a wife was an even worse fault on the part of Monsieur de Bernac, as this husband was called, for he could hardly be less accustomed to the pleasures of married life and it was far from likely that the strange habits which he substituted for the chaste and refined pleasures of conjugal existence would please a young person like Mademoiselle de Lurcie, the unfortunate girl whom Bernac had just linked to his fate. On their wedding night, after first making her swear that she would say nothing to her parents, he explained his preferences to his young wife; in the words of the famous Montesquieu, it was a question of that ignominious treatment which harks back to childhood: the young wife, assuming the posture of a little girl who has merited punishment, lent herself in this way for fifteen or twenty minutes to the brutal caprices of her elderly husband, and it was in the illusion created by this scene that he succeeded in enjoying that delightful intoxication of pleasure that any man with a more normal constitution than Bernac would certainly have wished to enjoy only in the arms of the delightful Lurcie.

The procedure seemed somewhat harsh to a sensitive pretty girl who had been brought up in comfortable circumstances and far from pedantry; however, since she had been told to be submissive she believed that all husbands behaved like this, perhaps Bernac had even encouraged her to believe so, and she lent herself in the most straightforward way possible to the depravity of her satyr-like husband; it was the same every day, and often more likely to be twice rather than once. After two years Mademoiselle de Lurcie, whom we shall continue to describe in this way, since she was still as virginal as on her wedding day, lost her father and her mother, and with them any chance of obtaining their help in the relief of her suffering, for which she had been hoping for some time.

This loss only made Bernac more enterprising, and if he had restrained himself to some extent during the lifetime of his wife's parents, now that she had lost them and it was impossible for her to beg anyone to avenge her, he lost all control. The treatment which at first had seemed no more than a joke gradually became real torment; Mademoiselle de Lurcie could not bear it, she became embittered and thought only of revenge. She saw very few people, for her husband isolated her as much as possible. However, the Chevalier d'Aldour, her cousin, in spite of all Bernac's representations, had never stopped seeing his young relative; this young man was extremely handsome and it was not without some purpose that he continued to visit his cousin. Since he was very well known in society the jealous husband, for fear of being laughed at, did not dare turn him out of the house too often. . . . Mademoiselle de Lurcie selected this relative to free her from the slavery in which she was living: she listened to the attractive propositions that her cousin put to her every day and in the end she confided in him completely, telling him everything.

'Avenge me on this horrible man,' she said to him, 'and avenge me by a scene so strong that he will never dare tell anyone about it: the day you succeed in this will be the day of your triumph, I shall be yours only at this price.'

D'Aldour was delighted, he agreed to everything and concentrated on the success of a venture which was to ensure him such pleasant moments. When everything was ready he spoke to Bernac.

'Sir,' he said to him one day, 'since I have the honour to be so closely related to you, and since I have such complete confidence in you, I must tell you about a secret marriage that I have just contracted.'

'A secret marriage!' said Bernac, delighted at finding himself freed in this way from the rival whom he feared.

'Yes, sir, I have just united myself to a charming wife and tomorrow she is to make me a happy man; she is a girl without property, I admit, but that is immaterial to me, I have enough for both of us; it is true that I am marrying the whole family, there are four sisters all living together, but since their company is pleasant it means only additional happiness for me. . . . I hope, sir,' the young man went on, 'that my cousin and you will do me the honour tomorrow of coming at least to the wedding breakfast.'

'Sir, I go out very little, and my wife even less, we both live a retired life, she enjoys it, I do not restrict her in any way.'

'I know your tastes, sir,' replied d'Aldour, 'and I assure you that all will be to your liking . . . I enjoy solitude as much as you do, in addition I wish to keep things secret, I told you so: it is in the country, the weather is fine, everything invites you, and I give you my word of honour that we shall be absolutely alone.'

Lurcie in fact indicated that she would like to go, her husband dared not oppose her in front of d'Aldour and the party was organised.

'Must you want such a thing?' said the complaining husband as soon as he was alone with his wife, 'you know very well that I don't care a fig for all this, I shall oppose all your wishes for outings of this sort, and I warn you that I plan shortly to send you to one of my estates where you will see nobody except me.'

And since this pretext, whether real or not, greatly enhanced the attractions of the lewd scenes which Bernac invented when the reality was lacking, he took advantage of the opportunity, made Lurcie go into her bedroom and said to her: 'We will go . . . yes, I promised to do so, but you shall pay dearly for the desire you showed for it. . . .'

The poor unhappy girl believed that she was nearing the end and tolerated everything without complaining.

'Do as you wish, sir,' she said humbly, 'you have shown me a favour, I owe you only gratitude.'

So much sweetness and resignation would have disarmed anyone except the libertine Bernac, whose heart was steeped in vice, but nothing stopped him, he took his pleasure, they went to bed quietly; the next day d'Aldour came as arranged to collect the husband and wife and they set out.

'You see,' said Lurcie's young cousin, taking them into an extremely isolated house, 'you see that this does not look much like a public celebration; not one carriage, not one lackey, I told you so, we are absolutely alone.'

Meanwhile four tall women of about thirty, robust, vigorous and all of them five feet six inches in height, came out on to the steps and advanced in a very civil way to receive Monsieur and Madame de Bernac.

'This is my wife, sir,' said d'Aldour, presenting one of them, 'and the other three are her sisters; we were married at dawn today in Paris and we are awaiting you in order to hold the nuptial feast.'

There were expressions of mutual politeness all round; after everyone had been together in the drawing-room for a moment, when Bernac convinced himself to his great satisfaction that he was just as much alone as he could possibly desire, a lackey announced that the wedding breakfast was served, and they went to table; nothing was gayer than this repast, and the four so-called sisters, who were very accustomed to jokes, revealed while at table all the vivacity and liveliness possible, but since decorum was not forgotten for one moment Bernac, who was thoroughly taken in, believed himself to be in the best company in the world; in the meantime Lurcie, who was delighted to see her tyrannical husband falling into the trap, joked with her cousin, and having decided out of despair that she would finally renounce the continence which so far had brought her nothing but sorrow and tears, tossed off champagne with him, overwhelming him with affectionate glances; the heroines, who needed to get their strength up, drank also, and Bernac, who was carried away, still suspecting only straightforward pleasure in such circumstances, hardly restrained himself any more than the rest of the company. But since it was important that no one should lose their self-control d'Aldour interrupted the proceedings in time and suggested that they should go to take coffee.

'Now, cousin,' he said to Bernac as soon as this was over, 'deign to come and see my house, I know you are a man of taste, I have bought it and furnished it expressly on the occasion of my marriage, but I fear I have made a bad bargain, you must please to give me your opinion.'

'With pleasure,' said Bernac, 'nobody understands these things better than I do, and I will estimate the value of the whole thing within ten louis, I wager.'

D'Aldour dashed to the staircase, giving his hand to his pretty cousin, Bernac was placed in the midst of the four sisters, and in this order they entered a very dark and isolated apartment, right at the end of the house.

'This is the bridal chamber,' said d'Aldour to the jealous old man, 'do you see this bed, cousin? That is where the bride will cease to be a virgin; is it not time after she has languished for so long?'

These words were the signal: at the same moment the four wily girls leapt upon Bernac, each one armed with a bundle of rods; they took his trousers off, two held him down and the other two took it in turns to belabour him.

'My dear cousin,' cried d'Aldour, 'didn't I tell you yesterday that you would be treated in the way you wanted? I couldn't think of any better way of pleasing you than by treating you in the same way as you treat this charming wife of yours every day; you are not barbarous enough to do anything to her that you would not like done to yourself, so I flatter myself that I am giving you pleasure; one thing is lacking still from the ceremony however, it is alleged that my cousin is still just as much a virgin, although she has been with you for so long, as though you were married yesterday; such neglect on your part can only be due to ignorance, I wager that you don't know how to set about it. . . . I am going to show you, my friend.'

And so saying, all to the sound of delightful music, the dashing man threw his cousin on the bed and made her a wife before the eyes of her unworthy husband. . . . At that moment only did the ceremony come to an end.

'Sir,' said d'Aldour to Bernac, as he came down from the altar, 'you may find the lesson somewhat forceful, but you must admit that the outrage was at least just as bad; I am not, and do not want to be your wife's lover, sir, there she is, I return her to you, but I advise you to conduct yourself more honourably with her in future; otherwise she would find in me an avenger who would spare you even less.'

'Madame,' said Bernac in a fury, 'this procedure really . . .'

'. . . is what you deserve, sir,' replied Lurcie, 'but if it displeases you, however, you have permission to spread it abroad, we shall each state our case and we shall see which one of us will make everyone laugh.'

Bernac was ashamed and acknowledged his faults; he invented no more sophistries to justify them, he threw himself at his wife's feet and begged her to forgive him: the sweet and generous Lurcie raised him up and kissed him, both of them went back home and I do not know how Bernac managed it, but from that moment Paris never saw a more intimate household, no married couple were ever so affectionate, loving and virtuous.

FLORVILLE AND COURVAL

Or Fatality

Monsieur de courval had just reached his fiftieth year; his youthfulness and good health could allow him to count on living another twenty years; having experienced only unhappiness with a first wife who had abandoned him a long time previously in order to devote herself to a libertine existence, and since evidence of the least equivocal kind led him to imagine that this creature was dead, he decided to make a second union with a reasonable person who, through a good character and an excellent way of life would succeed in making him forget his earlier misfortunes.

Monsieur de Courval had been as unfortunate in his children as in his wife; he had had only two, a daughter whom he had lost very young and a son who at the age of fifteen had abandoned him like his wife, unfortunately for the same life of debauchery; Monsieur de Courval, believing that nothing attached him to this unnatural son, planned as a result to disinherit him, and to give his possessions to the children he hoped to have by the new wife he wanted to take; he possessed an income of fifteen thousand livres, the result of his former employment in business, and he was spending it like an honest man along with some friends who liked him, all esteemed him and saw him sometimes in Paris, where he occupied a pleasant apartment in the rue Saint-Marc, and more often still in a charming little property near Nemours where Monsieur de Courval spent two-thirds of the year.

This honest man confided his plan to his friends, and, seeing that they approved of it, he begged them earnestly to look among their acquaintances for a person of about thirty to thirty-five, widowed or unmarried, who might suit his purpose.

Two days later one of his former colleagues came to tell him that he had definitely found someone suitable.

'The young lady whom I am offering you,' his friend told him, 'has two things against her, I should tell you about them first in order to console you afterwards by telling you about her good qualities; it is certain that she has neither father nor mother, but it is quite unknown who they were and where she lost them; what is known,' the intermediary continued, 'is that she is the cousin of Monsieur de Saint-Prât, a well-known man who admits this to be so, who esteems her and will sing you her praises in the least suspect and the best deserved way. She has inherited nothing from her parents but she has an annuity of four thousand francs from this Monsieur de Saint-Prât, in whose house she was brought up and where she passed all her youth: that is her first fault; let us go on to the second,' said Monsieur de Courval's friend: 'an intrigue when she was sixteen, a child who exists no longer and whose father was never seen again: that is all there is against her; now something in her favour.

'Mademoiselle de Florville is thirty-six years old, and appears barely twenty-eight; it would be difficult to have a more pleasant and interesting face: her features are sweet and delicate, her skin is as white as a lily and her auburn hair reaches to the ground; her fresh and pleasantly-shaped mouth is like a rose in springtime. She is very tall, but so well-formed, she moves so gracefully that her height, which otherwise might have made her look a little hard, is not noticeable; her arms, neck, legs and everything about her is shapely and her beauty is of the type which will not fade for a long time. As far as her conduct is concerned it is so orderly that it may perhaps displease you; she does not like society and lives in a very retired manner; she is very pious, very assiduous in her duties at the convent where she resides and if she edifies everyone round about her through her religious qualities she also delights everyone who sees her through her attractive mind and the charm of her character . . . in fact she is like an angel on earth preserved by Heaven for the happiness of your old age.'

Monsieur de Courval, delighted by such an encounter, hastily begged his friend to let him see the person in question.

'Her birth does not worry me,' he said, 'provided her blood is pure, what does it matter to me who transmitted it to her? Her romance at the age of sixteen alarms me just as little, she has made good this fault by many years of good conduct; I shall marry her as a widow, for since I have decided to take someone of thirty to thirty-five it would be difficult to add to this any absurd insistence on having a virgin, therefore nothing in your proposition displeases me, I can only urge you to allow me to see her.'

Monsieur de Courval's friend soon satisfied him; three days later he invited him to dinner at his house alone with the young woman in question. It was difficult not to be attracted at first sight by this charming girl; she had the features of Minerva herself, disguised beneath those of love. Since she knew what was at issue she was even more reserved and her modesty, reticence, the nobility of her demeanour, together with so many physical charms, such a gentle character, such a fair and well-stocked mind, went to poor Courval's head to such a degree that he begged his friend to be kind enough to hasten the conclusion.

They saw each other two or three times again, sometimes in the same house, at Monsieur de Courval's or at Monsieur de Saint-Prât's, and finally Mademoiselle de Florville, when earnestly pressed to state her feelings, declared to Monsieur de Courval that nothing flattered her so much as the honour he was good enough to show her, but that her delicacy did not allow her to accept anything before she had told him herself about the incidents of her life.

'You have not been told everything, sir,' said this

charming girl, 'and I cannot consent to be yours until you know more about it, and I would certainly not deserve it if, taking advantage of your delusion, I were to agree to become your wife without your judging if I am worthy to do so.'

Monsieur de Courval assured her that he knew everything, that it was his responsibility alone to formulate the anxieties she mentioned, and if he was fortunate enough to please her she should no longer be embarrassed about anything. Mademoiselle de Florville remained firm; she stated definitely that she would agree to nothing until Monsieur de Courval knew everything about her; so this became necessary; all that Monsieur de Courval could obtain was that Mademoiselle de Florville should come to his property near Nemours, that all arrangements should be made for the celebration of the marriage that he desired, and that once Mademoiselle de Florville's story had been heard, she should become his wife the next day.

'But, sir,' said this charming girl, 'if all these preparations should be useless, why make them? Suppose I persuade you that I was not born to belong to you?'

'That is something you will never prove, mademoiselle,' replied the honest Courval, 'that is something of which I defy you to convince me; so let us set off, I beg you, and do not oppose my plans.'

Nothing could be changed in these arrangements, all the preparations were made, and they left for Courval; they were however alone there, Mademoiselle de Florville had insisted on this; the things she had to say could only be revealed to the man who wanted to ally himself to her, and therefore nobody else was admitted; the day after she arrived, this beautiful and intriguing woman begged Monsieur de Courval to listen to her and told him the story of her life in the following terms:

Mademoiselle de Florville's Story

The intentions you have towards me, sir, no longer allow me to impose on you; you have seen Monsieur de

Saint-Prât, to whom you were told I was related, he himself has been good enough to support this statement, and yet from this point of view you have been deceived on all sides. Nothing is known about my birth, I have never had the satisfaction of knowing to whom I owed it. I was found, when I was a few days old, in a green taffeta cradle at the door of Monsieur de Saint-Prât's house, with an anonymous letter attached to the hood of my cradle, on which was written simply:

'You have no children after being married for ten years, you continually want some, adopt this one, her blood is pure, she is the product of the most chaste marriage and not of any libertine union, her birth is honourable. If the little girl does not please you, you should take her to the Foundling Hospital. Make no enquiries, none will succeed, it is impossible to tell you anything more.'

The honest people at whose house I had been left welcomed me at once, brought me up, took all possible care of me, and I can say that I owe them everything. Since there was no indication of my name it pleased Madame de Saint-Prât to call me Florville.

I had just reached my fifteenth year when I had the misfortune to lose my protectress; nothing can express the sorrow I felt at her death; I had become so dear to her that she begged her husband, on her death-bed, to guarantee me an annuity of four thousand livres and never to abandon me; these two conditions were executed at once, and in addition to these kindnesses Monsieur de Saint-Prât recognised me as a cousin of his wife's and made the contract that you have seen in this name. However I could no longer stay in that house, and Monsieur de Saint-Prât made me aware of this.

'I am a widower, and still young,' this virtuous man told me, 'living under the same roof will cause suspicions about us that we do not deserve; your happiness and your reputation are dear to me, I do not want to compromise either of them. We must separate, Florville; but I shall never abandon you for the rest of my life, I do not even want you to leave my family; I have a widowed sister at

Nancy, I shall send you there, I can guarantee that she will be as fond of you as I am, and there, where I can always keep my eye on you, so to speak, I can continue to look after all the needs of your education and settlement.'

I shed tears when I heard this news; this fresh sorrow renewed bitterly my recent grief at the death of my benefactress; I was however convinced that Monsieur de Saint-Prât's reasoning was correct, I decided to follow his advice and I left for Lorraine conducted by a lady of that district to whom I had been recommended and who left me in the hands of Madame de Verquin, Monsieur de Saint-Prât's sister, with whom I was to live.

Madame de Verquin's house was very different from that of Monsieur de Saint-Prât; in the latter there reigned modesty, religion and good living whereas I now saw that frivolity, love of pleasure and independence were the rule in the former establishment.

Madame de Verquin told me from the beginning that my prudish air displeased her, that it was unheard of to arrive from Paris with such an awkward demeanour and such ridiculous decorum, and that if I wanted to get on well with her I must adopt a different manner. This beginning alarmed me; I shall not try to appear better than I am, sir, but everything that is divorced from good living and religion has always displeased me so much throughout all my life, I have always been so opposed to anything that offended virtue, and the faults into which I have been drawn in spite of myself, have caused me so much remorse that it does me no service, I confess, to bring me back into society, I am not suited to live among others, they make me feel gloomy and withdrawn; the most obscure retreat is best suited to my state of mind and heart.

These ill-considered reflections, insufficiently developed at the age I was then, did not preserve me from the bad advice of Madame de Verquin, nor from the evils into which her seductions were to lead me; everything drew me in that direction, the company I saw all the time, the noisy delights with which I was surrounded, the examples and talk of the people, everything influenced me; they assured me I was pretty and to my misfortune I dared to believe them.

The Normandy regiment was garrisoned in this town at the time; Madame de Verquin's house was the officers' meeting-place; all the young women were to be found there too, and it was there that all the intrigues of the town were formed, broken and made up again.

It is likely that Monsieur de Saint-Prât knew nothing about some of this woman's conduct; how, in view of the austerity of his social life, would he have consented to send me to her house? This consideration held me back and prevented me from complaining to him; must I admit everything? Perhaps also I did not worry about it; the impure air that I breathed had begun to affect me, and like Telemachus on Calypso's island I would perhaps not have listened to the advice of Mentor.

Madame de Verquin, who had been shamelessly trying to seduce me for a long time, asked me one day if I had come to Lorraine with a free heart, and if I did not regret some lover in Paris?

'Alas, madame,' I told her, 'I have not even thought of committing the errors of which you accuse me, and your brother can answer for my conduct. . . .'

'Errors!' interrupted Madame de Verquin, 'if you have committed any it is that of being still too green for your age, I hope you will get over it.'

'Oh, madame, are these the words I should hear from a person so worthy of respect?'

'Respect? Oh, don't mention it, I assure you, my dear, that respect is of all feelings that which I am least concerned to inspire, it's love I want to inspire . . . but respect, I have not yet reached the age for that sentiment. Follow my example, my dear, and you will be happy. . . . Incidentally, have you noticed Senneval?' this siren went on, mentioning to me a young officer of seventeen who came fairly often to her house.

'Not particularly, madame,' I replied, 'I can assure you that I see them all with the same indifference.'

'But that's what you mustn't do, my young friend, in future I want us to share our conquests . . . you must have

Senneval, he's my creation, I took the trouble to train him, he loves you, you must have him. . . .'

'Oh, madame, please forgive me, I am really not interested in anyone.'

'You must be, this has been arranged with his colonel, who's my lover at the moment, as you can see.'

'I beg you to leave me free from this point of view, I have no inclination towards the pleasures you value.'

'Oh, you'll change, one day you'll enjoy them as I do, it's very simple not to value the things one hasn't yet experienced; but it is forbidden not to want to know the things that are made to be adored. In other words, the plans have been made; this evening, mademoiselle, Senneval will declare his passion to you, and you will please not to let him languish, or I shall be angry with you, but really angry.'

At five o'clock the company arrived; since it was very hot groups of people went out into the woods and everything was so well arranged that Monsieur de Senneval and I, finding ourselves to be the only ones who were not taking part, were forced to talk to each other.

It is useless to hide the fact from you, sir, no sooner had this pleasant and witty young man confessed his love than I felt myself drawn towards him by an uncontrollable impulse, and when later I tried to understand this feeling of sympathy, I found it completely obscure, it seemed to me that this inclination was by no means the result of an ordinary feeling, something concealed its nature from me; moreover, at the same time that my heart sped towards him, an invincible force seemed to hold it back, and in this chaos . . . in this ebb and flow of incomprehensible ideas, I could not make out if I was doing right to love Senneval or whether I should flee from him for ever.

He was given plenty of time to confess his love to me . . . alas, he was given only too much. I had every opportunity to reveal my sensitivity, he took advantage of my confusion, I was weak enough to tell him that he was far from displeasing me and three days later I was guilty enough to let him enjoy his victory.

The evil delight taken by vicious people in these triumphs over virtue is truly a strange thing; nothing equalled the transports of Madame de Verquin when she knew I had fallen into the trap she had prepared for me, she teased me and laughed, and assured me finally that what I had done was the most simple and reasonable thing in the world, and that I could receive my lover every night in her house without fear . . . that she would close her eyes to it; she was too occupied with her own affairs to worry about these trifles but she nevertheless wondered at my virtue, since it was likely that I would limit myself to one man, while she, if obliged to deal with three of them, would certainly remain far from my reserve and modesty; when I wanted to take the liberty of telling her that this irregularity was hateful, that it presupposed neither delicacy nor feeling, and that it reduced our sex to the lowest type of animal life, Madame de Verquin burst out laughing.

'Heroine of old France,' she said to me, 'I admire you and I don't blame you; I know very well that at your age delicacy and sentiment are the two gods to whom one sacrifices pleasure; it's not the same thing at my age, when one is completely blasé about these illusions, one grants them less importance; pleasures of a more material nature are preferable to the foolishness which appeals to you; and why should one be faithful to people who were never so to us? It is not enough to be the weaker without being the more deceived? A woman who brings delicacy of feeling into such conduct is quite absurd. . . . Believe me, my dear, vary your pleasures while your age and charms allow you to do so, and forget about your illusory constancy, a gloomy and uncivilised virtue, very unsatisfactory to oneself and which never triumphs over others.'

These remarks made me shudder, but I saw clearly that I no longer had the right to oppose them; the criminal attentions of this immoral woman were becoming necessary to me, and I had to treat her carefully; this is the fatal drawback of vice since it puts us, as soon as we yield to it, in the hands of people whom we would otherwise have despised, I accepted therefore all Madame de Verquin's blandishments; every night Senneval gave me new pledges of his love, and six months passed thus in such a state of intoxication that I barely had time to think.

Fatal consequences soon opened my eyes; I became pregnant and thought I would die of despair when I found myself in a condition which Madame de Verquin found amusing.

'All the same,' she told me, 'we must save appearances, and since it is not too respectable for you to have the baby in my house, the Colonel, Senneval and I have made some arrangements; the Colonel is going to give the young man leave, you will set off a few days before him for Metz, he will follow soon afterwards and there, supported by his presence, you will give birth to this illicit fruit of your love; afterwards you will return here one after the other as you left.'

I had to obey, I told you sir, you put yourself at the mercy of all men and all events when you have been unfortunate enough to commit a fault; you allow the whole world to acquire rights over you, you become the slave of every living creature, as soon as you have so far forgotten yourself as to become the slave of your passions.

Everything worked out as Madame de Verquin had said; on the third day Senneval and I were reunited at Metz at the house of a midwife whose address I had taken while leaving Nancy, and I gave birth to a son; Senneval, who had not ceased to show the most affectionate and delicate feelings, seemed to love me more since I had, as he said, enlarged his existence; he showed all possible consideration for me, begged me to leave him his son, swore to me that he would take the greatest possible care of him all his life, and did not think of reappearing at Nancy before fulfilling his duty towards me.

It was at the moment of his departure that I dared to make him realise to what point the fault he had made me commit was going to bring me unhappiness, and that I suggested it should be made good by uniting ourselves in front of the altar. Senneval had not expected this suggestion and became upset.

'Alas,' he told me, 'is it for me to say so? Since I am still a minor, would I not need my father's consent? What would become of our marriage if this formality had not been carried out? And besides, I am far from being a suitable match for you; as the niece of Madame de Verquin (in Nancy this was believed to be the case), you could aspire to something much better; believe me, Florville, let us forget our errors, and you may be assured of my discretion.'

These words, which I had been far from expecting, made me cruelly aware of the enormity of my error; my pride prevented me from replying, but my sorrow was all the more bitter; if anything had removed the horror of my conduct from my own eyes it had been, I admit, the hope of making it good by one day marrying my lover. Credulous girl that I was! I did not imagine, in spite of the perversity of Madame de Verquin, who should certainly have enlightened me, I did not believe that anyone could have found it amusing to seduce an unfortunate girl and abandon her afterwards, and this feeling of honour, this feeling so worthy of respect in the eyes of men, I did not imagine that it would fail to act in our case, and that our weakness could justify an insult that they would not dare to risk between themselves except at the cost of shedding blood. I saw myself therefore both as the victim and the dupe of him for whom I would have laid down my life a thousand times; this terrible reversal of feeling nearly drove me to my grave. Senneval never left me, his attentions were the same, but he never spoke to me again about my suggestion, and I was too proud to mention to him a second time the subject of my despair; in the end he disappeared as soon as he saw I had recovered.

I was determined not to return to Nancy any more, and feeling fully aware that I was seeing my lover for the last time in my life, all my wounds reopened at the moment of his departure; nevertheless I had the strength to bear this final blow . . . the cruel man! he left, he tore himself from my bosom which was drenched with my tears, but I did not see him shed a single one!

So that is what comes from these vows of love in which

we are foolish enough to believe! The more sensitive we are, the more do our seducers abandon us ... the traitors! They leave us because we have used additional means of keeping them.

Senneval had taken his child and placed him in a country district where it was impossible for me to discover him ... he had wanted to deprive me of the pleasure of cherishing and raising this tender outcome of our liaison; it looked as though he wanted me to forget everything that could still link us together, and I did so, or rather I thought I was doing so.

I determined to leave Metz at once and never to return to Nancy again; however, I did not wish to quarrel with Madame de Verquin; in spite of her errors she was close enough to my benefactor for me to treat her with consideration all my life; I wrote her the most honest letter in the world, and as a pretext for not reappearing again in the city I put forward my shame for the action I had committed and asked her permission to return to Paris to be near her brother. She replied to me at once that I was free to do anything I wished, that she would always be a friend to me. She added that Senneval had not yet returned, that they did not know where he was and that I was foolish to inflict all these miseries on myself.

After receiving this letter I returned to Paris and hastened to throw myself on my knees before Monsieur de Saint-Prât; my silence and my tears soon informed him of my misfortune; but I was careful enough to accuse myself alone, I never mentioned the seductions practised by his sister. Monsieur de Saint-Prât, like all people with good characters, had no suspicion concerning the misdeeds of his relatives and believed her to be the most honourable of women; I allowed him to keep all his illusions, and this conduct, of which Madame de Verquin was by no means unaware, preserved me her friendship.

Monsieur de Saint-Prât pitied me ... made me fully aware of my faults and finally forgave me.

'Oh my child,' he said, with that tender compunction of the honest-minded, so different from the hateful intoxication of criminals, 'oh, my dear daughter, you see what it costs to abandon virtue . . . it is so necessary to adopt it, it is so intimately linked to our existence, only ill-fortune remains to us when we abandon it; compare the tranquillity of your innocent state on leaving us with the terrible unhappiness in which you return. Do the meagre pleasures you have been able to enjoy during your fall compensate for the torments which now rend your heart? Happiness therefore lies only in virtue, my child, and all the sophistries of its detractors can never procure a single one of its delights. Ah, Florville, those who deny or oppose these so pleasant delights, do so only from jealousy, you may be sure, from the barbarous pleasure of making others as guilty and unhappy as they are. They are blind and would like everyone to be the same, they are mistaken, and would like everyone else to be mistaken; but if you could see into the depths of their hearts you would find only sorrow and repentance; all these apostles of crime are only evil and desperate people; you would not find one sincere person among them who would not admit, if he were truthful, that their poisonous words or dangerous writings had not been guided only by their passions. And what man in fact can say in cold blood that the bases of morality can be shaken without risk? What being would dare maintain that doing good and desiring good are not essentially the aim of mankind? And how can a man who will do only evil expect to be happy in a society whose strongest concern is the perpetual increase of good? But will not this apologist of crime not shudder himself when he has uprooted from all hearts the only thing which could lead to his conversion? What will stop his servants ruining him, if they have ceased to be virtuous? Who will prevent his wife from dishonouring him, if he has persuaded her that virtue is useless? Who will restrain his children if he has dared to blight the seeds of good in their hearts? How will his liberty and his possessions be respected if he has said to adults *impunity goes with you, and virtue is only an illusion?* Whatever the status of this unfortunate man, whether he be husband or father, rich or poor, master or slave, dangers will arise for him on all sides, and from all directions daggers will be held against his breast: if he has dared to destroy in men the only duties which compensate for his perversity, let us have no doubt, the unfortunate man will perish sooner or later, the victim of his terrible philosophy.*

Let us leave religion for a moment, if you will, let us consider only man; who would be stupid enough to believe that if he infringes all the laws of society the latter, after it had been outraged, could leave him in peace? Is it not in the interest of man, and in that of the laws he makes for his own safety, always to aspire towards the destruction of anything that hinders or hurts him? Some credit or wealth will perhaps ensure for the wicked man an ephemeral gleam of prosperity; but how short his reign will be! When he is recognised and unmasked and has soon become the object of hate and public disdain, will he then find either apologists for his conduct or supporters to console him? Nobody will want to accept him; since he will have nothing further to offer them, they will all reject him like a burden; surrounded by ill-fortune on all sides he will languish in opprobrium and wretchedness, and having been unable to take refuge even in his own heart he will soon die in despair.

'What therefore is this absurd reasoning on the part of our adversaries? What is this ineffectual attempt to belittle virtue, to dare to say that all that is not universal is illusory, and since virtues are only local none of them could be real? What, is there no virtue because every nation has had to create their own? Because different climates, different temperaments have necessitated different kinds of restraints, because, in a word, virtue has multiplied itself in a thousand different forms, is there no virtue in the world? One might as well doubt the reality of a river, because it divides into a thousand different streams. Well,

* Oh! my friend, never seek to corrupt the person whom you love, it can go further than you think, said a sensitive woman one day to a friend who wished to seduce her. Adorable woman, let me quote your own words, they depict so well the soul of her who soon afterwards saved this man's life, that I should like to engrave these moving words in the temple of memory, where your virtues guarantee you a place.

what better proof is there both of the existence of virtue and of its necessity than man's need to adapt it to all his different ways of life and to make it the basis of all of them? Show me a single race that lives without virtue, a single one among whom good deeds and humanity are not the fundamental bonds, I will go further, show me even a band of villains who are not kept together by some principles of virtue, and I renounce my cause; but if on the contrary it is shown to be useful everywhere, if there is no nation, no state, no society, no individual that can do without it, if man, in fact, cannot live happily or safely without it, would I be wrong, my child, in exhorting you never to relinquish it? See, Florville,' my benefactor went on, clasping me in his arms, 'see how far your first errors have caused you to fall; and should error tempt you again, if seduction or your weakness are likely to ensnare you again, think of the misfortunes caused by your first mistakes, think of the man who loves you like his own daughter . . . whose heart is rent by your faults, and you will find in these reflections all the strength demanded by the cultivation of the virtues, to which I wish to return you for ever.'

Monsieur de Saint-Prât, adhering to these same principles, did not open his house to me; but he suggested that I should go and live with one of his relatives, a woman as celebrated for the deep piety in which she lived as Madame de Verquin was for her immorality. This arrangement pleased me very much. Madame de Lérince accepted me with the greatest possible willingness and I was installed in her house the same week that I returned to Paris.

Oh, sir, what a difference between this respectable woman and her whom I had just left! If vice and depravity had established their rule with the latter, the heart of the former was the seat of all the virtues. I was just as comforted by her edifying principles as I had been frightened by the other woman's depravity: I had found only bitterness and remorse while listening to Madame de Verquin, I encountered nothing but sweetness and consolation in entrusting myself to Madame de Lérince. Ah, sir, allow me to depict to you this adorable woman, whom I shall love for ever;

my heart owes this homage to her virtues, it is impossible for me to resist it.

Madame de Lérince, aged about forty, was still very youthful, an air of candour and modesty embellished her features much more than the divine proportions with which nature had endowed her; a slight excess of nobility and modesty made her appear imposing at first, it was said, but what might have been taken for pride was softened as soon as she spoke; she had such a fine, pure heart, such perfect, such total frankness, that in spite of themselves everyone found that imperceptibly the veneration she inspired at first was followed by the most affectionate feelings. There was nothing exaggerated, nothing superstitious about Madame de Lérince's religion; with her the principles of faith were expressed through the most extreme sensitivity. The idea of the existence of God, the worship due to this supreme being, such were the deepest pleasures of this loving soul; she admitted aloud that she would be the most unfortunate of creatures if treacherous thinkers ever forced her mind to destroy the respect and love she had for her religion; even more attached, if it is possible, to the sublime morality of this religion than to its cult or ceremonies, she made this excellent morality the rule for all her conduct; never had calumny soiled her lips, she never even allowed herself to make a joke which might hurt anyone close to her; she was full of tenderness and sensitive feeling for her fellow creatures, finding people interesting, even as far as their faults were concerned, and her one preoccupation was either to hide their faults with care or else to reproach them gently on this account; if they were unhappy her greatest delight was to comfort them; she did not wait for poor people to come asking her for help, she sought them out . . . she guessed where they were, and you could see her face light up when she had consoled a widow or provided for an orphan, when she had spread ease in a poor family, or when she had broken the bonds of ill-fortune. There was nothing harsh or austere in all this; if chaste pleasures were offered to her she accepted them with delight, she even invented them, lest people around her became bored. Wise and enlightened with the moralist, profound with the theologian, she yet inspired the story-writer and smiled upon the poet, she astonished the legislator or the politician and would organise games for a child; she possessed every kind of wit, and its most noteworthy aspect was the particular care, the charming attention that she manifested either to bring out that of others or constantly to find it in them. Living a retired life from preference, cultivating her friends for their own sake, Madame de Lérince was in fact a model for both sexes and caused everyone close to her to enjoy that quiet happiness, that celestial pleasure promised to the honest man by the holy God in whose image she had been formed.

I shall not tire you, sir, with the monotonous details of my life during the seventeen years that I had the good fortune to live with this adorable creature. We divided our time between discussions on morality and piety and the greatest number of good deeds possible.

'Men only fail to become enthusiastic about religion, my dear Florville,' Madame de Lérince told me 'because clumsy guides make them aware solely of its restraints, without offering them its delights. Can there exist a man so absurd that in looking at the universe, he would have the audacity not to agree that so many marvels could only be the work of an all-powerful God?* Having become aware of this first truth . . . and does his heart need anything more in order to be convinced of it? . . . what sort of man is he then, this cruel and barbarous individual who could then refuse his homage to the beneficent God who created it? But the diversity of religions is embarrassing, one feels that their falsity lies in their quantity; what sophistry! Is it not in this unanimity of people to recognise and serve one god, is it not then in this tacit avowal which lies deep in all men's hearts that we can find even more strongly if possible than in the sublime works of nature, the irrevocable proof of the existence of this supreme god? Why, man cannot live without adopting a god, he cannot question himself without finding proofs of this within himself, he cannot open his eyes without finding everywhere traces of this god, and yet

* The use of the capital for 'God' follows the original.

he dares to doubt it! No, Florville, no, no true atheist exists; pride, obstinacy, the passions, these are the destructive weapons of this god who constantly comes to life again in the heart or the mind of man; and when each beat of this heart, when each luminous thought of this mind offers me this undeniable being, would I refuse him my homage, could I keep from him the tribute that his good allows my weakness, would I not humiliate myself before his greatness, would I not ask for grace and endure the miseries of life so that one day I could now take part in his glory? Would I not have the ambition to spend eternity in his bosom, or I would risk spending the same eternity in a fearful abyss of torture, for having refused to accept the indubitable proofs that this great being chose to give me of the certainty of his existence! My child, does this terrible alternative permit even a moment of reflection? Oh, all of you who obstinately reject the burning arrows cast by this same god into the depths of your hearts, be at least fair for one moment, and merely out of pity for yourselves, accept this invincible argument of Pascal: "if there is no God, what does it matter if you believe in him, what harm does this faith cause you? And if there is one, what dangers do you not run in refusing him your belief?" Incredulous men, you do not know, you say, what homage you should offer this god, the multiplicity of religions offends you; well then, examine all of them, I allow you to do so, then tell me afterwards in good faith which one reveals most greatness and majesty; deny, if it is possible, oh Christians, that the one in which you have had the good fortune to be born does not appear to you the one most holy and the most sublime characteristics: Look elsewhere for mysteries so great, for dogmas so pure, for a morality so consoling; find in another religion the ineffable sacrifice of a god, in favour of his creation; discover in any other finer promises, a more hopeful future, a god who is greater and more sublime! No, you cannot, philosopher of one day! you cannot do so, slave of your pleasures, whose faith changes with the physical state of your nerves; impious during the ardour of the passions, credulous as soon as they have subsided, you cannot, I tell you; feelings show it incessantly, this god whom your mind opposes, exists always beside you, even in the midst of your errors; break those chains that bind you to crime, and never will this holy and majestic god desert the temple erected to him in your heart. It is in the depths of your heart, oh, my dear Florville, that you must find the necessity for this god whose existence is indicated and proved to us by everything; it is from your heart also that you must also receive the necessity for the worship we pay him and it is this heart alone, which will convince you soon, dear friend, that the noblest and the purest of all is that in which we were born. Let us, therefore, practise with care and delight this gentle and consoling religion, may it fill the finest moments of our life on earth, and while we are led imperceptibly, still cherishing it, to the last moment of our life, may it be through a path of love and delight that we go to leave in the bosom of the eternal god this soul which emanates from him, created only in order to know him, and which we should have enjoyed only in order to believe in him and worship him.'

That is how Madame de Lérince spoke to me, that is how my mind was fortified by her advice, and how my soul became rarefied under her sacred wing; but as I told you, I am passing over in silence all the minor details of my life in this house, in order to tell you only what is essential; I should reveal my faults to you, generous and sensitive man that you are, and when heaven is good enough to allow me to live in peace along the path of virtue, I have only to express my thanks and be silent.

I had not stopped writing to Madame de Verquin, I received news from her regularly twice a month, and although I should no doubt have given up this correspondence, although my reformed life and higher principles constrained me in some way to sever it, my debt to Monsieur de Saint-Prât, and more than anything else, it must be said, a secret feeling which continually drew me towards the places where I had so many cherished links in the past, the hope perhaps of one day receiving news of my son, everything in fact let me continue a correspondence which

Madame de Verquin was good enough always to maintain with regularity; I tried to convert her, I extolled to her the delights of the life I was leading but she treated them as illusions, she continually laughed at my resolutions, or else she opposed them, and, remaining always constant about her own, she assured me that nothing in the world would be capable of weakening them, she described to me new proselytes whom it amused her to make and regarded them as much more docile than I had been; their repeated falls were, said this perverse woman, little triumphs that she never enjoyed without delight, and the pleasure of leading these young hearts towards evil consoled her for not being able to do everything that her imagination dictated to her. I often begged Madame de Lérince to lend me her eloquent pen in order to triumph over my adversary, and she agreed happily; Madame de Verquin would reply, and her sophistries, which were sometimes very strong, would oblige us to have recourse to arguments which triumphed over a sensitive soul in a very different way, and Madame de Lérince alleged, correctly, that they inevitably expressed everything necessary to destroy vice and confound disbelief. At the same time I asked Madame de Verquin for news of him whom I still loved, but either she could not or would not tell me anything.

The time has come, sir; let us speak of the second catastrophe of my life, this murderous incident which breaks my heart every time I think of it; learning of the horrible crime of which I am guilty will no doubt make you renounce the over-flattering projects that you have been forming on my behalf.

The house of Madame de Lérince, in spite of being so well-conducted, was however open to a few friends; Madame de Dulfort, a woman of a certain age, who had formerly been attached to the Princess of Piedmont and came to see us very often, one day asked Madame de Lérince's permission to introduce to her a young man who had been especially recommended to her, and whom she would be very happy to bring into a house where the examples of virtue that he would constantly see could only contribute to forming his character. My protectress made the excuse that she never entertained young men but, won over by her friend's earnest entreaties, she consented to see the Chevalier de Saint-Ange: he appeared.

Either a presentiment . . . or whatever you like to call it, sir, but when I set eyes on this young man, I shuddered all over and could not possibly understand why . . . I nearly fainted . . . I made no further attempt to understand the cause of this strange reaction, attributing it to some confusion in my mind, and Saint-Ange no longer made an impression on me. But if this young man had disturbed me in this way at first sight, he too had felt a similar effect . . . I learnt it finally from his lips. Saint-Ange was filled with such a great veneration for the house which had been opened to him that he dared not forget himself to the point of mentioning within it the passion that devoured him. Three months passed therefore before he dared to say anything to me about it; but his eyes expressed such ardour that it became impossible for me to be mistaken. Since I was determined not to fall once more into the kind of error which had caused the unhappiness of my life, and feeling much strengthened by better principles, I was twenty times on the point of warning Madame de Lérince of the feelings I thought I discerned in this young man; I was then restrained by the fear of making her afraid and decided to remain silent. A fatal resolution, no doubt, since it was the cause of the terrible misfortune that I shall now describe to you.

Every year we usually spent six months in a pleasant country estate owned by Madame de Lérince two leagues away from Paris; Monsieur de Saint-Prât often came to see us there; unfortunately for me gout kept him away that year, it was impossible for him to come; I say unfortunately for me, sir, because having naturally more confidence in him than in his relation, I would have told him things that I could never decide to tell others, and by admitting them I would no doubt have prevented the fatal accident which took place.

Saint-Ange asked Madame de Lérince for permission to

come with us, and since Madame de Dulfort also asked this favour on his behalf, it was granted to him.

All of us in the company were somewhat anxious to know who this young man was; nothing very clear or definite was known about his existence; Madame de Dulfort described him to us as the son of a gentleman in the provinces, from where she came; he, forgetting sometimes what Madame de Dulfort had said, passed himself off as a Piedmontese, a possibility that was fairly strongly supported by the way in which he spoke Italian. He did not serve in the army, but he was of an age to do something, and he had not yet made any decision about his future. He had moreover a very handsome face, and should have had his portrait painted; extremely decorous conduct, a straightforward manner of speaking, giving the impression of having had a good upbringing, but along with all this a prodigious vivacity, a kind of impetuousness in his character which sometimes frightened us.

As soon as Monsieur de Saint-Ange was in the country, it became impossible for him to hide from me the feelings which had only grown stronger through his attempts to restrain them; I shuddered . . . and yet became mistress enough of myself to show him only pity.

'Truly, sir,' I said to him, 'either you fail to recognise what you could value, or else you have a great deal of time to waste, in order to spend it with a woman twice your age; but supposing even that I was foolish enough to listen to you, what absurd ideas would you dare to entertain concerning me?'

'The idea of uniting myself to you by the most sacred union, mademoiselle; how little esteem you would have for me if you could imagine I would entertain any other!'

'Truly sir, I will not allow the public to see the extraordinary spectacle of a girl of thirty-four marrying a child of seventeen.'

'Ah, you are cruel, would you see this slight inequality if there existed in the depths of your heart one thousandth part of the passion that devours mine?'

'Indeed, sir, as far as I am concerned, I am very calm . . .
I have been so for many years, and I hope I shall be so as
long as it pleases God to let me languish in this world.'

'You remove from me even the hope of melting your
heart one day.'

'I shall go further, I dare forbid you to speak to me any
longer about your absurdities.'

'Ah, beautiful Florville, do you therefore want to bring
about the sorrow of my life?'

'I want you to have peace of mind and happiness.'

'All that can only exist with you.'

'Yes, . . . as long as you will not destroy absurd feelings
that you should never have conceived; try to conquer them,
try to be master of yourself, and your tranquillity will
return.'

'I cannot.'

'You do not want to, we must separate before you can
succeed; do not see me for two years, this effervescence will
subside, you will forget me and you will be happy.'

'Oh, never, never, happiness for me will be only at your
feet. . . .'

And since the company was about to rejoin us our first
conversation ended there.

Three days later Saint-Ange found the means of meeting
me alone once more and tried again to adopt the same tone
as on the previous occasion. This time I imposed on him a
silence so firm that he wept copiously; he left me suddenly,
telling me that I was driving him to despair and that he
would soon take his life if I continued to treat him in this
way . . . then he retraced his steps in a fury. . . .

'Mademoiselle,' he said to me, 'you do not know the heart
which you are outraging . . . no, you do not know it . . . ,
you must realise that I am capable of going to the farthest
extremes . . . , farther perhaps than you can imagine . . . ,
yes, I shall do so a thousand times over rather than
renounce the happiness of being yours.'

And he left in a state of terrible sorrow.

I was never more tempted than at this moment to speak
to Madame de Lérince, but I repeat to you, the fear of

causing harm to this young man restrained me, I kept silent. For a week Saint-Ange fled from me, he barely spoke to me, he avoided me at table . . . , in the drawing-room . . . , out on walks, and he did all this no doubt in order to see if this change in his behaviour would make any impression on me; if I had shared his feelings the method was certain of success, but I was so far from doing so that I hardly appeared to be aware of his manoeuvres.

At last he came up to me in the depths of the garden. . . .

'Mademoiselle,' he said to me, in the greatest state of violence . . . , 'I have finally succeeded in becoming calm, your advice has affected me in the way you expected it to . . . , you can see how composed I am now . . . , I have only tried to find you alone in order to take my leave of you . . . , yes, I am going to flee you for ever, mademoiselle, I am going to flee from you . . . , you will never see again the man whom you hate . . . , oh, no, no, you will never see him again.'

'This project pleases me, sir, I like to think that you are being reasonable at last; but,' I added, smiling, 'your conversion does not seem quite real to me yet.'

'Then how should I behave, mademoiselle, in order to convince you of my indifference?'

'Very differently from the way I see you now.'

'But at least when I have gone . . . , when you no longer have the displeasure of seeing me, perhaps you will believe that I have reached that state of reason to which you are trying so hard to bring me?'

'It is true that this alone will persuade me of it, and I shall continually advise you to adopt this course at once.'

'Ah, am I then such a terrible creature to you?'

'You are, sir, a very likeable man, who should hasten to make conquests of another kind, and to leave in peace a woman who cannot possibly listen to you.'

'But you shall hear me,' he said then in fury, 'yes, cruel woman, you shall hear, whatever you may say about it, the feelings of my passionate heart, and the assurance that there is nothing in the world that I shall not do, either to deserve you or to obtain you. . . . Do not believe at least,' he went on impetuously, 'do not believe in this feigned departure, I only feigned it in order to put you to the test . . . I leave you! . . . I tear myself away from the place where you are! I would rather suffer death a thousand times over! . . . hate me, perfidious woman, hate me, since such is my wretched lot, but never hope to conquer within me the love that consumes me for you.'

And Saint-Ange was in such a state as he uttered these last words, through a fatality that I have never been able to believe, he had succeeded so well in moving me that I turned away in order to hide my tears, and left him in the depths of the arbour where he had succeeded in finding me. He did not follow me; I heard him throw himself to the ground and abandon himself to the excesses of the most terrible delirium. . . . Even I, I must admit to you, sir, although I was quite certain I felt no love for this young man, either it was commiseration or memory, it was impossible for me not to break into sobs in my turn.

'Alas,' I said to myself as I yielded to my grief, 'this is what Senneval used to say to me . . . , it was in the same terms that he expressed his feelings of love to me . . . , also in a garden like this one . . . , did he not say that he would love me for ever . . . , and has he not cruelly deceived me! . . . Good heavens, he was the same age. . . . Ah, Senneval, is it you who seek to rob me of my tranquillity again? And are you not reappearing in this seductive guise in order to drag me once more into the abyss? Flee, coward, flee . . . , I hate even your very memory at the moment!'

I dried my tears and shut myself in my room until it was time for supper; then I went downstairs . . . , but Saint-Ange did not appear, he sent a message that he was ill, and the next day he was skilful enough to reveal nothing by his expression save tranquillity . . . , I was deceived by it; I really believed that he had made enough effort to control himself and conquer his passion. I was wrong; the traitor! . . . Alas, what am I saying sir, he deserves no more invectives . . . he deserves only my tears, he deserves only my remorse.

Saint-Ange only appeared so calm because he had made

his plans; two days passed like this, and towards the evening of the third he announced publicly that he was leaving; he made arrangements with his protectress, Madame de Dulfort, concerning their mutual affairs in Paris.

Everyone went to bed. . . . Forgive me, sir, for the way that the description of this terrible catastrophe upsets me in advance; I never remember it without making myself shudder in horror.

Since it was extremely hot I had thrown myself into bed almost naked; my chambermaid had gone, I had just put out my candle. . . . A work-bag unfortunately remained open on my bed, for I had just been cutting out gauzes that I needed the following day. My eyes had barely begun to close when I heard a sound . . . I sat up at once . . . I felt a hand seize hold of me . . .

'You shall escape me no more, Florville,' said Saint-Ange to me . . . it was he. . . . 'Forgive the excess of my passion, but do not try to escape it . . . you must be mine. . . .'

'Infamous seducer!' I cried, 'flee at once, or fear the effects of my wrath. . . .'

'I fear only that I shall not be able to possess you, cruel girl,' went on this ardent young man, leaping upon me so skilfully and in such a state of fury that I became his victim before I was able to prevent it. . . . Angry at such an excess of audacity, and decided on any course rather than to suffer the consequences, I thrust him away from me and seized hold of the scissors that lay at my feet; mistress of myself in spite of my fury, I tried to find his arm in order to strike it and frighten him by this resolution on my part rather than to punish him as he deserved; as he felt the movement I made he redoubled his own violence.

'Flee, traitor!' I cried, striking him as I thought in the arm, 'and blush at your crime. . . .'

Oh, sir, a fatal hand had directed my blows . . . the unfortunate young man uttered a cry and fell to the ground. . . . Lighting my candle again at once I went up to him . . . he was dying! I threw myself on this bleeding corpse . . . I clasped it wildly against my heaving bosom . . . I pressed my mouth against his in an attempt to revive a soul that was dying; I washed his wound with my tears. . . .

'Oh, you whose only crime was to love me too much,' I said with the distraction of despair, 'do you deserve such suffering? Must you lose your life through the hand of her to whom you would have sacrificed your own? Oh, unhappy young man . . . , image of him whom I once adored, if only love is needed to restore you to life, learn, at this cruel moment, when alas you can no longer hear me . . . learn if your heart still beats, that I want to bring you back to life at the cost of my own . . . , learn that you were never indifferent to me . . . , that I never saw you without being upset, and that the feelings I had for you were perhaps much deeper than the faint love which burned in *your* heart.'

With these words I collapsed lifeless on the body of this unfortunate young man; my chambermaid, who had heard the noise, came in, looked after me, united her efforts with mine to restore Saint-Ange to life. . . . Alas, all was unavailing. We left that fatal apartment, locking the door carefully, we took away the key and rushed that moment to Paris to the house of Monsieur de Saint-Prât . . . I caused him to be awakened, I gave him the key to that fatal room, I told him of my horrible escapade, he pitied me, he consoled me, and ill though he was, he went at once to Madame de Lérince's house; since her country estate was very near Paris all these events took place during the night. My protector arrived at his relative's house just as everyone was rising, and nothing had yet transpired; never did friends and relatives conduct themselves better than on this occasion; far from imitating those stupid or ferocious people whose only pleasure in such crises is to noise abroad all that can damage or upset both themselves and those about them, the servants barely suspected what had occurred.

'Well, sir,' said Mademoiselle de Florville at this point, interrupting herself, because of the tears which choked her, 'will you now marry a woman capable of such a murder? Will you tolerate in your arms a creature who has merited the rigours of justice? An unfortunate woman in fact whose crime torments her incessantly, who has not spent a single peaceful night since that cruel moment? No, sir, not one has passed without my unfortunate victim appearing to me bathed in the blood which I had shed.'

'Calm yourself, mademoiselle, calm yourself, I beg you,' said Monsieur de Courval, who wept in sympathy with this touching girl; 'nature has given you a sensitive soul and I understand your remorse; but there is not even a hint of crime in this fatal adventure, it was certainly a horrible misfortune, but no more than that; nothing premeditated, nothing atrocious, merely the desire to escape from the most unpleasant attack . . . , a murder in fact committed by chance in defending yourself. . . . Reassure yourself mademoiselle, reassure yourself, I demand that you do so; the most severe court would do no more than dry your tears; oh, how mistaken you were if you feared that such an incident would deprive you of all the rights over my heart that your qualities ensure you. No, no, beautiful Florville, this incident, far from dishonouring you, makes your virtues shine brighter, it only makes you more worthy of finding a consoling hand to help you forget your sorrows.'

Monsieur de Saint-Prât, continued Mademoiselle de Florville, also had the goodness to say what you have told me; but the excessive kindness you have both shown does not silence the reproaches of my conscience, nothing will stifle my remorse. No matter, let us go on, sir, you must be anxious about the outcome of all this.

Madame de Dulfort was no doubt heartbroken; this young man, who was very interesting in his own right, had been too highly recommended to her for her not to mourn his loss; but she understood the reasons for silence, she saw that publicity, in causing my ruin, would not restore life to her protégé, and remained silent. Madame de Lérince, in spite of her austere principles, and the excessive regularity of her way of life, behaved even better, if that were possible, because prudence and humanity are the distinctive characteristics of true piety; first she let it be known in the house that I had been foolish enough to want to go back to Paris during the night in order to enjoy the coolness of the weather, that she was perfectly aware of this slight imprudence; that in any case I had acted rightly for her own plan had been to go there for supper the same evening, and on this pretext she sent all her servants there. Once she was alone with Monsieur de Saint-Prât and her friend, they sent for the curé; Madame de Lérince's pastor must have been a man as wise and intelligent as she was; he gave a correct certificate to Madame de Dulfort without any difficulty and along with two of her servants gave a secret burial to the unfortunate victim of my fury.

As soon as these tasks had been fulfilled all the servants came back, everyone was sworn to secrecy, and Monsieur de Saint-Prât came to calm me, telling me of all that had been done to consign my error to the greatest possible oblivion; he seemed to want me to return as usual to Madame de Lérince's . . . she was ready to receive me . . . , I could not accept the responsibility; he therefore advised me to take some distraction. Madame de Verquin, with whom I had never ceased to remain in contact, as I told you sir, still pressed me to go and spend some months with her, I mentioned this plan to her brother, he approved it and a week later I left for Lorraine; but the memory of my crime pursued me everywhere, nothing succeeded in calming me.

I used to wake up in the middle of the night, thinking I could still hear the groans and cries of the unfortunate Saint-Ange, I could see his blood-stained body at my feet, I heard him reproach me for my barbarous conduct, assuring me that the memory of this terrible deed would pursue me until the end of my days, and that I did not know the heart I had rent asunder.

One night, Senneval, the unfortunate lover whom I had not forgotten, since he alone still drew me to Nancy . . . , Senneval appeared to me in a dream and showed me two bodies, that of Saint-Ange and that of a woman unknown to me,* he wept over both of them and indicated a coffin

* The reader should not forget the expression: . . . A woman unknown to me, so that he will not become confused. Florville has still to suffer some losses, before the veil is lifted, allowing her to recognise the woman she saw in the dream.

bristling with thorns which seemed to lie open in readiness for me; I woke in terrible agitation, confused feelings crowded into my mind, a secret voice seemed to say to me: 'Yes, as long as you live, this unfortunate victim will make you shed tears of blood, which each day will become more scalding; and the arrows of remorse will grow continually sharper instead of becoming blunted.'

It was in this state, sir, that I reached Nancy, and endless new sorrows awaited me there; when once the hand of fate weighs down upon us, its blows always crush us with redoubled force.

I came to Madame de Verquin's house, she had begged me to do so in her last letter, and said that it would be a pleasure to see me again; but great heavens, in what conditions were we both to enjoy this pleasure! When I arrived she was on her death-bed, who could have said so, she had written to me only two weeks earlier . . . , telling me of the things she was enjoying just then and of those that would follow; this is what happens to the plans of humans, it is when they make them in the midst of their pleasures that death cuts the thread of their days without pity, and in the midst of life, without ever concerning themselves with this fatal moment, living as though they were to exist for ever, they disappear into the obscure cloud of immortality, uncertain of the fate which lies in store for them.

Allow me, sir, to interrupt for a moment the story of my adventures in order to tell you of this loss and to describe to you the terrible stoicism which accompanied this woman to the tomb.

Madame de Verquin, who was no longer young—she was then fifty-two years old—after a party which was absurd at her age, jumped into the water in order to cool down, felt ill, was carried back home in a terrible state and the next day she had a congestion of the lungs; six days later she was told she had barely twenty-four hours to live. This news did not frighten her at all; she knew that I was going to come, she asked that I should be received; I arrived, and according to the doctor's pronouncement, she should have died that same evening. She had caused herself to be placed in a room furnished in the most tasteful and elegant way possible; she had lain down there, informally attired, on a voluptuous bed hung with lilac-covered curtains attractively decorated with real flowers; bunches of carnations, jasmine, tuberoses and roses decorated every corner of the apartment, a basketful of them stood beside her, both her room and her bed were covered with them.

'Come close, Florville,' she said, 'embrace me on my bed of flowers . . . , how tall and beautiful you have grown . . . , oh, indeed my child, virtue has done you good . . . , you have been told of my state . . . , you have been told, Florville . . . , I am aware of it also, in a few hours, I shall no longer be alive; I had not thought that I would be seeing you for such a short time . . . ,' and as she saw my eyes fill with tears she said, 'come now, silly girl, don't behave like a child . . . , do you think I'm unhappy then? Have I not enjoyed life as much as any woman in the world? I am losing only the years during which I should have had to renounce pleasure, and what would I have done without that? In fact I don't complain at all of not having lived to old age; in a few years' time no man would have wanted me, and I have never wanted to live after the time when I inspired only disgust. Death is only to be feared, my child, by those who believe; always between hell and paradise, they are uncertain which one will open for them, and this anxiety breaks their hearts; as for me, who have no hopes, and who am quite sure of not being more unhappy after my death than I was during my life, I shall fall asleep quietly in the bosom of nature, without regret as without pain, without remorse as without anxiety. I have asked to be buried under my jasmine arbour, the place has already been prepared for me, I shall be there, Florville, and the atoms emanating from my body after its destruction will serve to nourish and germinate the flower I have loved more than any others; you know,' she went on, tapping my cheeks with a spray of the same blooms, 'you will breathe in from them the soul of your former friend; as they spring up towards the fibres of your brain they will give you delightful ideas, they will force you to think of me still.'

My tears began to flow again . . . , I clasped the hands, of this unhappy woman, and wanted to exchange these frightening materialistic ideas for some less impious systems of thought, but hardly had I expressed this desire than Madame de Verquin repulsed me with horror. . . .

'Oh, Florville,' she cried, 'I beg you not to poison my last moments with your false beliefs, and let me die in peace; I have not detested them all my life in order to adopt them at the moment of my death. . . .'

I fell silent; what could my poor eloquence have achieved against such determination? I should have broken Madame de Verquin's heart without converting her, and humanity prevented me from doing this; she rang the bell, and at once I heard sweet and melodious music, which seemed to come from a neighbouring room.

'This,' said this epicurean woman, 'is how I want to die; Florville, is this not better than being surrounded with priests who would fill my last moments with confusion, alarms and despair? No, I want to teach your pious friends that one can die peacefully without being like them, I want to convince them that it is not religion we need before we can die in peace, but only courage and reason.'

It was getting late: a notary whom she had summoned entered; the music ceased, she dictated some of her wishes; she had no children and, having been a widow for several years, was the owner of many possessions; she made legacies to her friends and her servants, then she took a small casket from a secretaire that stood near her bed.

'This is all that is left to me,' she said, 'a little money and a few jewels. Let us entertain ourselves for the rest of the evening; there are six of you in my room, I am going to divide this into six lots, we'll have a lottery, you will draw lots between yourselves and take what falls due to you.'

I could not accustom myself to this woman's attitude, it seemed to me incredible to have so many things with which to reproach oneself and to reach one's last moment with such calm, the fatal effect of disbelief; if the horrible end of some wicked people is terrifying, how much more frightening is such a sustained resistance.

However, her wishes were carried out; she caused a splendid collation to be served, partook of several dishes and drank Spanish wines and liqueurs, the doctor having said that in the state she was this would make no difference.

Lots were drawn, each of us received about a hundred louis either in gold or in jewels. This little game was barely over when she was seized by a violent attack.

'Well, is it now?' she said to the doctor, still with the greatest calm.

'I fear so, madame.'

'Come then, Florville,' she said to me, holding out her arms to me, 'receive my last farewells, I want to die in the bosom of virtue . . .' she clasped me firmly against her, and her beautiful eyes closed for ever.

Since I was a stranger in this house and there was no longer anything to keep me there, I left immediately, you can imagine in what state . . . and how this scene had made me feel even gloomier than before.

Madame de Verquin's way of thinking was too far removed from mine for me to love her sincerely; was it not moreover the first cause of my dishonour and of all the setbacks that had followed it? Yet this woman, the sister of the one man who had really taken care of me, had had only excellent intentions towards me, she even continued to shower me with them while dying; I wept sincerely therefore and my bitterness redoubled as I reflected that, in spite of possessing excellent qualities, this unhappy creature had involuntarily destroyed herself; and that, rejected already by the etérnal God, she was no doubt suffering cruelly from the punishment incurred by a life so depraved. God's supreme goodness nevertheless came to me, in order to calm these heart-breaking thoughts; I went down on my knees, I dared to pray to the supreme being to pardon this unfortunate woman; I who needed the pity of Heaven so much, I dared to implore it for others, and in order to sway it as much as was in my power I added two louis of my own money to the sum I had won in Madame de Verquin's lottery and immediately caused it all to be distributed to the poor of the parish.

As far as other things were concerned, the intentions of this unfortunate woman were carried out exactly; she had made the arrangements too carefully for them to go wrong; she was laid in her jasmine arbour, on which one single word was engraved: VIXIT.

So perished the sister of my greatest friend; Madame de Verquin was full of wit and knowledge, possessing also endless graces and talents, and if her way of life had been different, she could have earned the esteem and love of everyone who knew her; she obtained only their contempt. Her irregularities increased as she grew older; women with no principles are never more dangerous than at the age when they have ceased to blush; depravity poisons the heart, they commit their first errors with refinement, and come imperceptibly to crime, believing still that they are only committing errors; but the incredible blindness of Madame de Verquin's brother did not cease to surprise me: such is the distinctive sign of innocence and goodness; honest people never suspect evil of which they are incapable themselves, and that is why they are so easily taken in by the first rogue who gets hold of them, which explains why it is so easy and so inglorious to deceive them; the insolent knave who tries to do so succeeds only in debasing himself, and without even having proved his talents for vice he has only enhanced the glory of virtue.

In losing Madame de Verquin I lost all hope of receiving any news of my lover and my son, you can easily imagine that I had not dared to mention them to her in the terrible state in which I had seen her.

Overwhelmed by this catastrophe, exhausted by a journey made in a terrible state of mind, I decided to rest for a time at Nancy, at the inn where I was staying, without seeing anyone whatsoever, since Monsieur de Saint-Prât had apparently wanted me to keep my name a secret there; it was from there that I wrote to this beloved protector, having decided that I would only leave after he had replied.

'An unfortunate girl who is nothing to you, sir,' I said to

him, 'who deserves only your pity, continually disturbs your existence; instead of speaking to you about the sorrow which you must be feeling about your recent loss, she dares to speak to you about herself, to ask you for your orders and to await them, etc. . . .'

But it was ordained that misfortune would follow me everywhere and that I would be perpetually either the witness or the victim of its sinister effects.

One evening I came back fairly late, after taking the air with my chambermaid, for I was accompanied only by this girl and a hired lackey, whom I had taken on when I arrived in Nancy; everyone had already gone to bed. As I was going to my room, a woman of about fifty, tall and still handsome, whom I had known by sight since I had been lodging in the same house, came suddenly out of the room next to mine and, armed with a dagger, went into another room opposite. . . . Naturally I watched . . . I flew after her and my servants followed me; in the twinkling of an eye, before we had time either to call or to help, . . . we saw this wretched creature hurl herself upon another woman, plunge her weapon twenty times into her heart and return to her own room with a distracted look, incapable of seeing us. We thought at first that the creature had taken leave of her senses; we could not understand a crime for which we could see no motive; my chambermaid and my servant wanted to call out; but a stronger urge, which I could not understand, forced me to make them remain silent, seize them by the arm and take them with me into my apartment, where we immediately locked the doors.

There was soon a terrible commotion; the woman who had just been wounded with the dagger had thrown herself as best she could on to the staircase, uttering horrible cries; she had had time, before dying, to name the woman who had killed her; and since it was known that we were the last to return to the inn we were arrested at the same time as the guilty woman. Since the dying woman's words had none the less left no suspicion concerning us we were merely forbidden to leave the inn until the end of the trial. The criminal was dragged to prison but admitted nothing and defended herself firmly; there were no other witnesses except my servants and myself, we had to appear . . . we had to speak, I had to conceal carefully the anxiety which was secretly devouring me . . . I, who deserved to die like the woman whom my forced admissions were going to send to her death, since I was guilty, in different circumstances, of a similar crime. I would have given anything in the world in order to avert these harsh depositions; as I dictated them I felt that every word I spoke was like a drop of blood wrung from my heart; however, everything had to come out, we admitted what we had seen. In spite of any convictions the court may have had about the crime committed by this woman, who stated that she had assassinated her rival, whatever certainty there was, I say, about this crime, we heard definitely afterwards that without us she could not possibly have been sentenced, because there was a man involved who escaped and who might well have been suspected; but our admissions, especially those of the hired lackey, who belonged to the inn and was attached to the place where the crime had taken place, these cruel statements, which we could not refuse to make without compromising ourselves, sealed the fate of this unfortunate woman.

At our last meeting, this woman shuddered violently, looked at me and asked my age.

'Thirty-four,' I told her.

'Thirty-four? And do you come from this province?'

'No, madame.'

'Is your name Florville?'

'Yes,' I replied, 'that is what I am called.'

'I do not know you,' she went on; 'but you are honest, well regarded, they say, in this town; unfortunately that is enough for me. . . .'

Then she went on in a state of confusion:

'Mademoiselle, I had a dream about you in the midst of all this horror; you were with my son . . . for I am a mother and unhappy, as you can see . . . you had the same face . . . the same figure . . . the same dress . . . and the scaffold was before my eyes. . . .'

'A dream,' I cried . . . 'a dream, madame'—and as my own came back to me this woman's features struck me, I recognised her as the one who had appeared to me with Senneval, by the coffin bristling with thorns. . . . My eyes filled with tears; the more I looked at this woman the more I was tempted to denounce myself . . . I wanted to ask if I could die instead of her . . . I wanted to flee and could not tear myself away. . . . When other people saw the terrible state into which she was driving me, since they were convinced of my innocence, they contented themselves with separating us; I went back to the inn exhausted, overwhelmed with a host of different feelings of which I could explain the cause, and the next day the wretched woman was led to her death.

The same day I received Monsieur de Saint-Prât's reply; he asked me to come back. Since Nancy was not likely to be very pleasant for me after these fateful scenes I left it at once for the capital, pursued yet again by the new phantom of this woman who seemed to cry out to me every second: *it is you, unhappy woman, it is you who are sending me to my death, and you do not know whom your hand is leading there.*

Overwhelmed by so many scourges, persecuted by an equal number of sorrows, I begged Monsieur de Saint-Prât to find me some retreat where I could end my days in the most profound solitude, carrying out the strictest duties of my religion; he suggested to me the place where you found me, sir; I settled there the same week and only left it to come twice a week to visit my beloved protector and in order to pass a few moments with Madame de Lérince. But heaven, which sent me hard blows every day, did not allow me to enjoy the company of this dear friend for long, I was unfortunate enough to lose her last year; she was so affectionate towards me that I did not want to separate from her at these harsh moments, and it was in my arms also that she breathed her last.

But who would have thought it, sir? this death was not as tranquil as that of Madame de Verquin; the latter, having never hoped for anything, had no fear of losing everything; Madame de Lérince seemed to shudder at seeing the certain object of her hope vanish; I had seen no remorse in the woman whom it should have struck deeply . . . whereas she who had never needed to feel any, became aware of it. Madame de Verquin, as she died, only regretted that she had not done enough harm, while Madame de Lérince expired repenting of the good she had left undone. The former decked herself with flowers, deploring only the loss of her pleasures; the latter wanted to die upon an ashen cross, heart-broken at the memory of the hours that she had not devoted to virtue.

These contrasts made a deep impression on me; I relaxed a little and asked myself why in such moments tranquillity appears to be enjoyed not by the good but by those whose behaviour has been bad? But that same moment, strengthened by a heavenly voice which seemed to ring out in the depths of my heart, is it for me, I cried, to probe the wishes of the eternal God? What I see ensures for me one additional merit: Madame de Lérince's fears are the concerns of virtue, Madame de Verquin's cruel apathy is only the last irregularity of crime. Ah, if I am able to choose my last moments, may God rather do me the favour of frightening me like the latter rather than of rendering me insensible like the former.

Such was truly the last of my adventures, sir; I have been living at the Convent of the Assumption for two years, where my benefactor placed me. Yes, sir, I have been there two years, never finding a single moment of rest, never spending a single night without the image of the unfortunate Saint-Ange and that of the unhappy woman whom I condemned at Nancy appearing before my eyes; that is the state in which you found me, there are the secret facts that I had to reveal to you; was it not my duty to tell you of them before yielding to the feelings that abuse you? . . . Can she whose soul is broken with sorrow bring some happiness into your life? Ah, believe me, sir, cease to have any illusions; allow me to return to the austere retreat which alone is suitable for me; if you were to wrest me from it this would only lead to the perpetual and terrible spectacle of remorse, sorrow and misfortune.

Mademoiselle de Florville came to the end of her story in a state of violent agitation. Since she was by nature emotional, lively and sensitive it was impossible for the account of her misfortunes not to have affected her considerably.

Monsieur de Courval, who found no plausible reasons, either in the earlier or later incidents in this story, for changing his plans, employed all his powers to calm the woman he loved.

'I repeat, mademoiselle,' he told her, 'there are fatal and strange occurrences in what you have just told me; but I do not see one which is liable to upset your conscience or harm your reputation . . . an intrigue at the age of sixteen . . . I admit it, but what excuses you had . . . your age, Madame de Verquin's policy of seduction . . . a young man who was perhaps very likeable . . . , whom you have not seen again, have you mademoiselle?' went on Monsieur de Courval with some anxiety . . . 'whom you will probably never see again.'

'Oh never, most certainly,' replied Florville, guessing the reasons for Monsieur de Courval's anxiety.

'Well, mademoiselle, let us bring matters to a conclusion,' the latter went on, 'I beg you to finish, and let me convince you as soon as possible that there is nothing in your story which can ever reduce in the heart of an honest man either the extreme consideration due to so much virtue, nor the homage due to so many charms.'

Mademoiselle de Florville asked permission to return to Paris again to consult her protector for the last time, promising definitely that no obstacle would arise on her side. Monsieur de Courval could not refuse this honest duty; she left, and returned a week later with Monsieur de Saint-Prât. Monsieur de Courval overwhelmed the latter with honours; he showed him as clearly as he could how flattered he was to unite himself to the woman whom he condescended to protect, and begged that he would continue to grant the title of relative to this likeable person; Saint-Prât replied as he should to Monsieur de Courval's attentions and continued to give him the most satisfactory impression of Mademoiselle de Florville's character.

At last the day so desired by Monsieur de Courval arrived, the ceremony took place, and on reading the contract he was very surprised to find that on the occasion of this marriage, Monsieur de Saint-Prât, without telling anyone, had added four thousand livres of income to the amount that he already paid as an allowance to Mademoiselle de Florville, and a legacy of one hundred thousand francs payable on his death.

This attractive girl wept copiously when she learned of her protector's fresh generosity, and was in fact glad that she could offer the man who was good enough to think of her a fortune at least equal to that which he possessed already.

Graciousness, pure joy and reciprocal assurances of esteem and attachment presided over the celebration of this marriage . . . this fateful marriage, whose torches were secretly extinguished by the furies.

Monsieur de Saint-Prât spent a week at Courval, and so did the friends of the newly-wed pair, but the husband and wife did not follow them to Paris, they decided to remain in the country until the beginning of winter, in order to settle their affairs in such a way that they could have a good house in Paris. Monsieur de Saint-Prât was asked to find them an attractive house near to his own, so that they could see each other more often, and in the happy expectation that these pleasant arrangements would be made Monsieur and Madame de Courval had already spent nearly three months together; there was already proof that the wife was pregnant, and they had at once told the good Saint-Prât about this when an unforeseen incident cruelly dashed the happiness of the married pair and changed the delicate roses of their union into ghastly wreaths of cypress.

At this juncture my pen comes to a halt . . . I should ask my readers for mercy, beg them not to read any further . . ., yes . . ., yes . . . let them stop at once if they do not want to shudder with horror. . . . How sad is man's condition in the world . . . how harsh are the strange effects of fate. . . . Why must the unhappy Florville, the most virtuous, the most likeable and the most sensitive creature, find herself to be, through an inconceivable sequence of fatal events, the most appalling monster whom nature ever created?

One evening this affectionate and lovable wife was seated by her husband, reading an English novel of incredible grimness, which at the time was causing a great stir.

'Indeed,' she said, throwing the book down, 'this creature is almost as unhappy as I am.'

'As unhappy as you!' said Monsieur de Courval, clasping his dear wife in his arms, 'Oh, Florville, I thought I had made you forget your misfortunes . . . , I can see that I was mistaken . . . must you tell me so harshly!'

But Madame de Courval appeared to have become unconscious, she replied not a word to her husband's caresses, with an involuntary movement she repulsed him with horror and rushed away, throwing herself on a distant sofa, where she burst into tears; in vain did this honest husband kneel beside her, in vain did he beg the wife whom he adored to calm herself or at least to tell him the reason for such a fit of despair; Madame de Courval continued to repulse him and to turn away when he tried to dry her tears, to such a point that Courval no longer doubted that a fatal memory of Florville's former passion had returned to arouse her again, and could not refrain from making some reproaches to her on the subject; Madame de Courval heard them without replying, but finally she rose to her feet.

'No, sir,' she said to her husband, 'no . . . , you are mistaken in interpreting my fit of despair in this way, it is not memories that alarm me, but presentiments . . . I am happy with you, sir . . . yes, very happy . . . and I was not born to be so; it is impossible for me to be so for long, the fatality of my star is such that for me the dawn of happiness is only the lightning that precedes the thunder . . . and that is what makes me shudder, I fear that we are not destined to live together. Today I am your wife, tomorrow perhaps I shall be so no longer. . . . A secret voice cries in the depth of my heart that all this happiness is only an illusion for me, which will fade like a flower that blooms and dies in a day. Do not accuse me therefore of capriciousness nor of coldness, sir, I am guilty only of too great an excess of sensitivity, only of an unfortunate gift for seeing everything on the black side, the cruel result of my setbacks. . . .'

Monsieur de Courval, kneeling at his wife's feet, tried to calm her by his caresses, by his words, but without success, when all at once . . . it was about seven o'clock in the evening, during the month of October . . . a servant came to say that a stranger was asking insistently to see Monsieur de Courval . . . Florville shuddered . . . , involuntary tears furrowed her cheeks, she staggered, she tried to speak but her words died on her lips.

Monsieur de Courval, who was more occupied with his wife's condition than with what he was being told, replied sharply that the man must wait; he flew to help his wife but Madame de Courval, fearing that she would succumb to the hidden impulse that was influencing her . . . trying to hide her ordeal from the stranger who had been announced, rose firmly and said:

'It is nothing, sir, nothing, let him come in.'

The lackey went out, returning a moment later followed by a man of thirty-seven or thirty-eight, his face, which was moreover pleasant, revealing signs of the deepest sorrow.

'Oh, my father,' cried the unknown man, throwing himself at the feet of Monsieur de Courval, 'will you recognise an unfortunate son who has been separated from you for twenty-two years, who has been punished too harshly for his cruel errors by the setbacks which have not ceased to overwhelm him during that time?'

'Who, you, my son . . . great Heavens! . . . how . . . ungrateful man, what can have reminded you of my existence?'

'My heart . . . , this guilty heart which nonetheless never ceased to love you . . . , listen, my father, listen, I have greater misfortunes than mine to reveal to you, condescend to sit down and listen to me, and you, madame,' the young Courval went on, addressing his father's wife, 'forgive me if at the first time in my life that I pay my respects to you, I find myself obliged to lay bare before you

(132)

terrible family misfortunes which it is no longer possible to conceal from my father.'

'Speak, sir, speak,' stammered Madame de Courval, glancing at the young man with distracted eyes, 'the language of sorrow is not new to me, I have known it since my childhood.'

Then the traveller looked fixedly at Madame de Courval and answered her with a kind of involuntary agitation:

'You, unhappy . . . madame . . . oh great heavens, you could not be as unhappy as we are!'

They sat down . . . Madame de Courval was in an almost indescribable state . . . , she gazed at this man . . . , she looked down . . . , she sighed in agitation . . . Monsieur de Courval wept, and his son tried to calm him, begging him to pay attention. At last the conversation took a calmer turn.

'I have so much to tell you, sir,' said the young Courval, 'that you must allow me to omit details in order to recount only the facts; and I demand both you and your wife to give me your word that you will not interrupt until I have finished telling you everything.

'I left you at the age of fifteen, sir, my first instinct was to follow my mother whom I was blind enough to prefer to you; she had been separated from you for many years; I rejoined her in Lyons, where her misdemeanours alarmed me to such a point that in order to preserve the remaining feelings I had for her I found myself forced to flee from her. I went to Strasbourg where the Normandy regiment was stationed. . . .'

Madame de Courval became upset, but contained herself.

'I inspired some interest in the Colonel,' the young Courval continued, 'I made myself known to him, he made me a sub-lieutenant, the following year I came with the corps to the garrison in Nancy; I fell in love there with a relative of Madame de Verquin, I seduced this young person, I had a son by her and I abandoned the mother cruelly.'

At these words Madame de Courval shuddered, a subdued moan rose to her lips, but she still remained firm.

'This unfortunate adventure was the cause of all my misfortunes, I placed the child of this luckless young lady in the care of a woman near Metz, she promised to look after him and shortly afterwards I returned to my corps; my conduct was criticised, and since the young lady could not reappear in Nancy, I was accused of having caused her ruin; she was too attractive not to have found many admirers all over the town and some among them acted as her avengers; I fought a duel, I defeated my adversary, I returned to Metz, took my son and went to Turin with him. I served the King of Sardinia for twelve years. I shall not mentioned the misfortunes I suffered there, they are legion. When you leave France you miss the country. However, my son grew up and promised extremely well. At Turin I met a Frenchwoman who had accompanied the French princess who married into the royal family there, and since this respectable person had taken an interest in my misfortunes, I dared to suggest to her that she should take my son to France in order to perfect his education, promising her that I would put my own affairs sufficiently in order for me to take him off her hands in six years' time; she accepted, neglected nothing for the good of his education and sent me very accurate news about him.

I returned a year earlier than I had expected, I arrived at this lady's house, full of the sweet consolation of being able to embrace my son, to clasp in my arms this pledge of a feeling that had been betrayed but which still consumed my heart. . . . 'Your son is no longer alive,' this worthy friend told me, shedding tears, 'he has been the victim of the same passion that caused his father's misfortune; we took him to the country, he fell in love there with a charming girl whose name I have sworn to keep secret; carried away by the violence of his love he wanted to snatch by force what the virtuous girl refused him; a blow which was only intended to frighten him penetrated his heart and killed him.'

At this point Madame de Courval fell into a kind of daze which made them fear for a moment that she might have lost her life completely; her eyes had a fixed stare, her blood was frozen. Monsieur de Courval, who grasped only too well the fatal connection between these unhappy adventures, interrupted his son and flew towards his wife ... she recovered, and with heroic courage spoke to him:

'Let us allow your son to continue, sir,' she said, 'perhaps I have not yet come to the end of my misfortunes.'

Meanwhile the young Courval, who understood nothing of this lady's sorrow at facts which seemed to concern her only indirectly, but discerning something incomprehensible in the features of his father's wife, gazed at her continually with emotion; Monsieur de Courval seized his son's hand and, distracting his attention from Florville, told him to continue, to mention only essentials and to leave out details, because these narratives contain mysterious details which become vastly interesting.

'In despair at the death of my son,' the traveller went on, 'having no longer anything to keep me in France ... except you alone, my father! ... whom I dared not approach, and whose wrath I fled, I decided to travel in Germany. ... Unhappy father, this is the harshest thing I still must tell you,' said the young Courval, bathing his father's hands in tears, 'I beg you to take courage.'

'On arriving at Nancy, I learned that a certain Madame Desbarres—that is the name my mother had assumed during her period of misconduct, as soon as she had made you believe she was dead—I learned, as I said, that this Madame Desbarres had just been sent to prison for having stabbed her rival, and that she would probably be executed the next day.'

'Oh, sir,' cried the unhappy Florville at this point, throwing herself into her husband's arms with tears and piercing cries. ... 'Oh, sir, do you see all the result of my misfortunes?'

'Yes, madame, I see everything,' said Monsieur de Courval, 'I see everything, madame, but I beg you to allow my son to finish.'

Florville said no more, but she could hardly breathe, not one of her feelings was unaffected, while every nerve underwent a terrible contraction.

'Go on, my son, go on,' said the unfortunate father; 'in one moment I shall explain everything to you.'

'Well, sir,' the young Courval went on, 'I enquired if there were no misunderstanding over the names; it was unfortunately only too true that this criminal was my mother, I asked to see her, obtained permission to do so and fell into her arms. "I am dying guilty," this unfortunate woman told me, "but there is a terrible fatality in the incident which leads me to my death; another person would have been suspected, he would have been, all the evidence was against him, a woman and her two servants who happened to be in that inn by accident saw my crime, but I was too preoccupied to notice them; their testimony is the sole cause of my death; no matter, let us not waste the few moments I have to speak to you in vain lamentations; I have important secrets to tell you, listen to them, my son. As soon as my eyes are closed, you must go and find my husband and tell him that among all my crimes there is one of which he has never known, and which I must at last confess. . . .'

' "You have a sister, Courval . . . , she came into the world a year after you . . . , I adored you, I was afraid that this sister would cause harm to you and that when it was necessary to arrange a marriage for her one day the fortune that should have belonged to you would be reduced; in order to preserve it more intact for you, I decided to get rid of this daughter, and to take all steps to ensure that in future my husband would have no more children from our marriage. My disordered way of life led me into other misdemeanours and prevented these new crimes from having other effects by making me commit further ones that were more terrible; but as far as this daughter was concerned, I determined without pity to put her to death; I was going to carry out this infamous deed in co-operation with the nurse, whom I was rewarding amply, when this woman told me that she knew a man who had been married for many years, had constantly desired children and could not have any; she would get rid of my child for me without committing a crime and in a way that might make her happy; I agreed at once. My daughter was taken that very night to this man's door with a letter in her cradle; hasten to Paris, as soon as I have ceased to live, beg your father to forgive me, not to curse my memory, and to take this child back to his home."

'With these words my mother kissed me . . . and sought to calm the terrible distress into which I had been cast by what she had told me. . . . Oh, my father, she was executed the next day. A terrible illness brought me near to the tomb, I have spent two years hovering between life and death, possessing neither the strength nor the courage to write to you; the first result of my return to health is that I come to throw myself at your feet, to beg you to forgive this unhappy wife, and to tell you the name of the person from whom you will have news of my sister; he is Monsieur de Saint-Prât.'

Monsieur de Courval was upset, all his senses froze, his faculties grew blunt . . . his condition became terrible.

As for Florville, who had seemed shattered for the last quarter of an hour, she rose with the calmness of someone who has just made a decision.

'Well, sir,' she said to Courval, 'do you now believe that anywhere in the whole world there can exist a criminal more terrible than the wretched Florville? . . . Recognise me, Senneval, recognise at the same time your sister, the girl whom you seduced in Nancy, your son's murderer, your father's wife and the hateful creature who dragged your mother to the scaffold. . . . Yes, gentleman, those are my crimes; wherever I look I see only an object of revulsion; either I see my lover in my brother or I see my husband in my father, and if I look at myself I see only the unspeakable monster who stabbed her son and sent her mother to her death. Do you believe that Heaven can hold enough torments for me, or do you suppose that I can survive for one moment the scourges that lacerate my heart? No, there is still one crime I must commit, this one will avenge all the others.'

And that very moment the wretched woman leapt upon one of Senneval's pistols, impetuously drew it and shot herself before anyone had time to guess her intention. She died without uttering another word.

Monsieur de Courval lost consciousness, his son, who was overwhelmed by so many horrible scenes, called for help as best he could; it was no longer necessary for Florville, the shadows of death were already spreading over her face, her shattered features revealed only the impact of violent death and the convulsions of despair . . . she lay in her own blood.

Monsieur de Courval was carried to his bed, he stayed there for two months at death's door; his son was in an equally wretched state but was nevertheless fortunate enough for his affection and help to recall his father to life; but both of them, after the blows of fate had been so cruelly multiplied, decided to withdraw from the world. An austere solitude removed them for ever from the eyes of their friends, and there, in the bosom of piety and virtue, they both found a peaceful end to a sad and distressing life, which had been granted to them solely in order to convince both them and those who will read this tragic story, that it is only in the obscurity of the tomb that man can find calm, the calm which the wickedness of their fellows, the unruliness of their passions and, more than anything else, the fatality of their destiny, will always forbid them enjoying on earth.

THE HUSBAND WHO PLAYED PRIEST

A Provençal Tale

Between the town of Menerbe in the county of Avignon and that of Apt in Provence stands the small isolated Carmelite monastery of St. Hilaire, situated on a mountain slope where even the goats can hardly find a foothold; this little place acts as a sewer for all the neighbouring Carmelite communities, each one of them consigns to it anyone who has brought dishonour upon them, from which it is easy to deduce how pure the society of such a house must be: drunkards, frequenters of prostitutes, gamblers, of such, more or less, is its noble composition, recluses who in this scandal-haunted refuge offer to God as best they can hearts that the world no longer wants. One or two neighbouring châteaux and the town of Menerbe, which is only one league from St. Hilaire, constitute the entire society of these good monks who, in spite of their habit and their calling are however far from finding all doors in the neighbourhood open to them.

For a long time Father Gabriel, one of the saints in this hermitage, had coveted a certain woman in Menerbe whose husband, a cuckold if ever there was one, bore the name of

Monsieur Rodin. Madame Rodin was a little brunette of twenty-eight whose roguish eye and nicely curving hips seemed to constitute her from all points of view a toothsome morsel for a monk. As for Monsieur Rodin, he was a good man, who cultivated his garden without saying a word: he had sold cloth, he had been a provost, and was therefore what is called an honest bourgeois; being not too sure whether his better half was virtuous, he was however philosophical enough to feel that the real way of combating an excessive growth of cuckold's horns was to give the impression of not suspecting that he had sprouted them; he had studied for the priesthood, he spoke Latin as well as Cicero and very often played draughts with Father Gabriel, who, as a skilful and farsighted courtier knew that if one wants a woman one must always woo her husband slightly. Father Gabriel was a real stallion among the children of Elias: one might have said that the entire human race could happily have entrusted him with the work of propagating them; a giver of babies if ever there was one, with firm shoulders, a back as broad as an ell, a dark swarthy face, eyebrows like Jupiter's, he was six feet tall and possessed that attribute which is particularly characteristic of the Carmelites, resembling, apparently, that of the best mules in the province. What woman could fail to be drawn to such a lustful specimen? He was therefore singularly attractive to Madame Rodin, who was very far from finding such sublime qualities in the good man whom her parents had given her as a husband. Monsieur Rodin appeared to close his eyes to everything, as we have mentioned, yet he was no less jealous for all that, he said not a word, but he stayed where he was, and he stayed at moments when the others would often have liked him to be miles away; but the time was ripe all the same. The naïve Madame Rodin had simply told her lover that she was only waiting for an opportunity to respond to desires which seemed too ardent to be resisted any longer, and on his side Father Gabriel had made Madame Rodin realise that he was ready to satisfy her. . . . During a brief moment when Rodin had been obliged to go out Gabriel had even shown his attractive mistress things which make up a woman's mind for her if she is still slightly doubtful . . . therefore only the opportunity was lacking.

One day Rodin came to ask his friend from St. Hilaire to dinner, intending to suggest that they went out shooting, and after they had drunk a few bottles of Lanerte wine, Gabriel thought this moment was a propitious occasion for the satisfaction of his desires.

'Zounds, sir provost,' said the monk to his friend, 'how pleased I am to see you today, you couldn't have come at a better time for me, I have some business of the greatest importance in which you're going to be remarkably useful.'

'What is it, father?'

'Do you know a man called Renoult in your town?'

'Renoult the hatter?'

'Precisely.'

'Well?'

'Well, the devil owes me a hundred écus and I have just heard that he's on the verge of bankruptcy, he may even have left the country by now. . . . I must absolutely rush over there to see him, and I can't.'

'Why not?'

'Because of Mass, damn it, I have to say Mass, I wish the Mass could go to the devil and that I had the hundred écus in my pocket.'

'But can't you be let off?'

'Let off, that would be fine! There are three of us here, and if we didn't say Mass three times every day the Father Superior, who never says it himself, would report us to Rome; but there is a way of helping me, my good man, see if you can consider it, it's up to you.'

'Oh, I'm willing all right, what do I have to do?'

'I'm alone here with the sacristan; after the two earlier Masses have been said, our monks have already gone out, nobody will suspect the trick, there won't be many people, a few peasants and at the most perhaps that very devout little lady who lives at the Château of . . . half a league away, an angelic creature who hopes that she can make up for all her husband's frivolity through her own austere conduct; I think you told me that you'd studied for the priesthood?'

'Indeed I did.'

'Well, you must have learnt how to say Mass.'

'I say it like an Archbishop.'

'Oh, my dear good friend,' Gabriel went on, throwing his arms round Rodin's neck, 'for heaven's sake, put on my habit, wait until eleven o'clock strikes, it's ten now, and then say Mass for me, I beg you; the brother who is sacristan is a good fellow and will never give us away; if anyone says they didn't recognise me we'll say it was a new monk, the others can be left in the dark. I'll dash over and see that devil Renoult, I'll get my money or kill him, and I'll be back in two hours. Wait for me, you can grill the soles, crack the eggs, draw the wine; when I'm back we'll have dinner and go out hunting . . . yes, my friend, I think we'll have good hunting this time: they say that a horned beast has been seen round here lately, I'm damned if we won't get him, even if we let ourselves in for twenty lawsuits with the local squire!'

'Your plan's a good one,' said Rodin, 'and I can assure your there's nothing I wouldn't do to help you, but wouldn't it be sinful?'

'Don't say a word about sin, my friend, it might perhaps be sinful if the thing was done and done badly, but in doing it without authorisation there's no difference between saying Mass and saying nothing. Believe me, I'm a casuist, there's nothing in this procedure that could be called mortal sin.'

'But must I say the words?'

'Why not? There's no virtue in those words except when we say them, but also it's so much in us . . . you see, my friend, if I said those words over your wife's body I would transform the temple where you carry out the sacrifice into a god. . . . No, no, my good man, we are the only ones who have the power to bring about transubstantiation; you could repeat the words twenty thousand times without causing God to descend; even with us the operation often falls completely flat, faith achieves everything, with a scrap of faith you can move mountains, Jesus Christ said so, but without faith you can achieve nothing. . . . Take me, for example, sometimes when I say Mass I'm thinking rather more about the girls and women in the church than about that devilish piece of wafer that I'm handling, do you think that I could summon anything then. . . . I would rather believe in the Koran than get that idea into my head. So your Mass will be practically as good as mine: therefore, my good man, have no scruples and above all, take heart.'

'Hang it,' said Rodin, 'I'm as hungry as a hunter, and it's still two hours to dinner time!'

'What's to stop you having a bite, here you are, have some of this.'

'And what about the Mass I've got to say?'

'Good heavens, what are you worrying about, do you believe that God comes to any more harm by falling into a full stomach rather than an empty one? Whether food is above or below, the devil take me if it isn't the same thing; don't worry, old fellow, if I went to Rome to say so every time I dine before saying Mass I'd spend my life on the road. And since you're not a priest, our rules cannot bind you, you're only going to give an impression of Mass, you're not going to say it; so you can do anything you want before or afterwards, you can even kiss your wife if she were there, you only have to do as I do, you don't have to celebrate or consummate the sacrifice!'

'Very well, then,' said Rodin, 'I'll do it, don't worry.'

'Good,' said Gabriel, departing hastily, after leaving his friend with a strong recommendation to the sacristan. . . . 'You can count on me, my dear man, I'll be with you before two o'clock,' and the delighted monk vanished.

Naturally he arrived without delay at Rodin's house; the provost's wife was surprised to see him, since she believed him to be with her husband, and asked him the reason for such an unexpected visit.

'Let's be quick, my dear,' said the breathless monk, 'let's be quick, we only have a moment to ourselves . . . give me a glass of wine and then let's get down to it.'

'But what about my husband?'

'He's saying Mass.'

'Saying Mass?'

'Yes, dammit, yes, my darling,' replied the Carmelite, pushing Madame Rodin on to the bed, 'dear heart, I've made your husband into a priest and while the rogue is celebrating a divine mystery let us quickly consummate one that is profane. . . .'

The monk was vigorous; he was difficult to resist when he took hold of a woman: his reasons moreover were so demonstrative that he convinced Madame Rodin and since he did not find it tedious to convince a roguish girl of twenty-two* with a Provençal temperament, he renewed his demonstrations more than once.

'But my darling,' said the lovely creature at last, when she was entirely convinced, 'do you know that time presses . . . we must separate: if our pleasure is only to last as long as a Mass it should have reached the stage of *Ite missa est* a long time ago.'

'No, no, my dear,' said the Carmelite, who had one more argument to put to Madame Rodin, 'come on, sweetheart, we've got plenty of time, once more, my love, once more, those novices don't go as fast as we do . . . once more, I tell you, I wager the cuckold hasn't got to the end yet.'

They had to separate however, not without promising to meet again, they agreed on a few deceptions, then Gabriel went to find Rodin; the latter had celebrated Mass as well as a bishop.

'It was only the *quod aures* which worried me a bit,' he said, 'I wanted to eat instead of drink, but the sacristan put me right. And what about the hundred écus, Father?'

'I've got them, my son; the devil tried to say no, I took hold of a fork and I can tell you I belaboured him on his head and all over.'

The gathering came to an end, however, the two friends went out hunting and on his return Rodin told his wife about the service he had performed for Gabriel.

'I was celebrating Mass,' said the silly man, laughing heartily, 'yes, dammit, I was celebrating Mass like a real

* See page 140; this is an inconsistancy in the original.

curé while our friend was beating Renoult over the head with a fork. . . . He hit him, my love, just fancy that, he banged him on the forehead; what a funny story, old girl, and how cuckolds make me laugh! And what were you up to while I was celebrating Mass, my dear?'

'You know, love,' his wife replied, 'it looks as though heaven has been inspiring us, just see how celestial things were occupying both of us without our suspecting it: while you were saying Mass, I was reciting that beautiful prayer with which the Virgin replied to Gabriel when he came to announce to her that she would conceive through the Holy Ghost. Don't worry, my friend, we'll certainly be saved, as long as we're both occupied with doing such good deeds.'

EMILIE de TOURVILLE
or The Cruel Brothers

NOTHING IS SO SACRED within a family as the honour of its members, but if this treasure becomes tarnished, however precious it may be, should those who have an interest in defending it do so at the cost of burdening themselves with the humiliating role of persecuting the unfortunate creatures who offend them? Would it not be reasonable to set against them the horrors with which they torment their victim and the harm, often imaginary, which they claim to have suffered? In short, who is more guilty from the viewpoint of reason, a weak daughter who has been deceived, or a relative who, in setting himself up as the avenger of a family, becomes the murderer of this unfortunate girl? The story that we are about to present to our readers will perhaps resolve the question.

The Comte de Luxeuil, a lieutenant-general, a man of about fifty-six or fifty-seven, was returning by post-chaise from one of his properties in Picardy when, passing through the forest of Compiègne, at about six o'clock in the evening on a day near the end of November, he heard the cries of a woman which seemed to be coming from the corner of one of the paths lying near the highway that he was crossing; he stopped and ordered his valet de chambre, who was running beside the chaise, to go and see what it was. He was told that it was a young girl of about sixteen or seventeen, covered in blood, which made it impossible to see where she was hurt, and who was asking for help. The Comte immediately left his chaise and rushed to the unfortunate girl. He also found it difficult, because of the darkness, to see from where she was bleeding, but from her replies he realised at last that it was from the veins in the arms usually used for bloodletting.

'Mademoiselle,' said the Comte, after helping the girl as much as he could, 'I am not in a position to ask you the cause of your misfortunes, and you are hardly in a state to tell me: come into my carriage, I beg you, and our only concern now will be to calm you and for me to help you.'

And so saying Monsieur de Luxeuil, assisted by his valet de chambre, carried the poor young lady into the post-chaise and they set off.

No sooner had this intriguing person seen herself to be in safety than she tried to stammer out some words of thanks, but the Comte begged her not to speak.

'Tomorrow, mademoiselle, tomorrow, you will tell me I hope all that concerns you, but today, through the authority granted over you by my age and the good fortune I have in being useful to you, I urgently ask you to think only of calming yourself.'

They arrived; in order to avoid scandal, the Comte had his protégée wrapped in man's cloak and told his valet de chambre to take her to a convenient apartment at the far end of his house. He went to see her as soon as he had received the embraces of his wife and son who were both expecting him for supper that evening.

When the Comte went to see the invalid he took a surgeon with him; the latter examined the young lady and found her in a state of indescribable exhaustion, the paleness of her face almost made it appear that she had barely a few moments to live, but she had no wounds; her weakness, she said, was due to the vast amount of blood that she had been losing every day for three months, and as she was about to tell the Comte the unnatural cause of this prodigious loss, she collapsed, and the surgeon declared that she must be kept calm and merely given restoratives and cordials.

The unfortunate young woman passed a fairly good night but for six days she was not in a state to instruct her benefactor about the events which had affected her; on the evening of the seventh day, finally, when everyone in the Comte's household were still unaware that she was concealed there, and she herself, through the precautions that had been taken, did not know where she was, she begged the Comte to hear her and above all to show indulgence, no matter what errors she would confess. Monsieur de Luxeuil took a chair, assured his protégée that he would never lose interest in her, for she was made to inspire it, and in this way our beautiful adventuress began the story of her misfortunes.

The story of Mademoiselle de Tourville

I am the daughter, sir, of the Président de Tourville, who is too well known and too distinguished in his profession to be unknown to you. For two years after leaving the convent I never went out of my father's house; since I had lost my mother while very young he alone took care of my education and I can say that he neglected nothing in order to give me all the graces and charms of my sex. These attentions, the plans that my father announced for arranging the best possible marriage for me, perhaps even a slight predilection, all this soon awoke the jealousy of my brothers, one of whom had been a judge in a provincial court for three years and had just attained his twenty-sixth year while the other, more recently made a counsellor, was soon to be twenty-four.

I did not imagine that I was as deeply hated by them as I have reason to know today; having done nothing to deserve such feelings on their part I was under the pleasant illusion that they returned those which my heart innocently formed for them. Oh, heavens, how mistaken I was! Apart from the time given to my education I enjoyed the greatest possible liberty in my father's house, for, making me solely responsible for my conduct he restricted me in no way, and for the last eighteen months I had even had permission to walk in the mornings with my chambermaid either on the terrace of the Tuileries or on the rampart nearby where we lived, and also to go with her either on foot or in one of my father's carriages to visit my friends or my women relatives, provided that this was not at a time when a young person can hardly be alone in the midst of a group of older people. The entire cause of my misfortunes lies in this fatal liberty, that is why I mention it to you, sir, would to God I had never had it.

A year ago, while walking, as I have just told you, with my chambermaid, who is called Julie, in a shaded alley of the Tuileries, where I believed I was more solitary than on the terrace, and where I felt the air was clearer, six young ruffians came up to us and indicated through their dishonourable remarks that they took us for prostitutes. I was horribly embarrassed by such a scene and, not knowing how to escape, I was about to seek salvation in flight when a young man whom I was accustomed to see often walking alone at more or less the same times as myself, and whose appearance showed him to be entirely honest, happened to pass by while I was in this trouble.

'Sir,' I cried, calling him over to me, 'I have not the honour of being known to you, but we see each other here nearly every morning; what you have seen of me must have convinced you, I flatter myself, that I am not an adventuress; I beg you earnestly to assist me by taking me back home and delivering me from these bandits.'

Monsieur de ...., you will allow me to keep his name a secret, for only too many reasons oblige me to do so—immediately ran up, he sent away the ruffians who surrounded me, convinced them of their mistake by the air of politeness with which he greeted me, took my arm and at once led me from the garden.

'Mademoiselle,' he said to me shortly before reaching our door, 'I think it is wise to leave you here; if I take you back home, it will be necessary to explain the reason; this might lead to your being forbidden to go out for walks alone any more; conceal therefore what has just happened, and continue to come here as you usually do in this same alley, since it entertains you and your family allow you to do so. I shall not fail to come there every single day and you will find me always ready to lay down my life, if necessary, to prevent you from being disturbed.'

An offer so obliging made me look at this young man with a little more interest than I had thought of doing previously; finding him two or three years older than me and possessing a charming appearance. I blushed as I thanked him, and the ardent features of this god-like seducer, who is the cause of my present misfortune, penetrated right to my heart, before I had time to resist him. We separated, but I thought I could see from the way in which Monsieur de .... left me that I had made on him the same impression that he had just made on me. I returned to my father's house, I took care to say nothing and went back the next day to the same alley, spurred on by a feeling that was stronger than myself, which would have made me brave any danger which could have been encountered ... what I am saying, I might perhaps have sought them, in order to have the pleasure of being saved from them by the same man ... I am describing my soul to you, sir, perhaps too naïvely, but you promised to be indulgent to me and each new development in my story will make you see that I need this; this is not the only rash thing you will see me do, this is not the only time when I shall need your pity.

Monsieur de .... appeared in the alley six minutes after me, and came up to me as soon as he saw me:

'Dare I ask you, mademoiselle,' he said, 'if yesterday's incident caused no scandal, and if you did not suffer as a result?'

I assured him not, and told him that I had taken advantage of his advice, that I thanked him for it and flattered myself that nothing would disturb the pleasures found in coming to take the morning air in this fashion.

'If you find it pleasant, mademoiselle,' replied Monsieur de .... in the most honourable way, 'those who are fortunate enough to meet you there no doubt enjoy it more, and if I took the liberty of advising you yesterday not to risk anything which might upset your walks, in fact you owe me no thanks for it: I dare to assure you, mademoiselle, that I said this not so much for you as for me.'

And as he said this he looked at me so expressively . . . oh, sir, why should it be to this soft-spoken man that I owed my later misfortunes! I replied honestly to his remark, conversation began, we walked round twice and Monsieur de . . . . did not leave me without entreating me to let him know to whom he had been fortunate enough to render service the previous day; I did not think I should conceal this from him, he also told me who he was and we separated. For nearly a month, sir, we did not cease to see each other in this fashion nearly every day, and this month did not pass without us confessing to each other what we felt, and without swearing to each other that we would feel this way forever.

Finally Monsieur de . . . . begged me to let him see me in a place less restricting than a public park.

'I do not dare present myself to your father, my beautiful Emilie,' he said to me. 'Since I have never had the honour of knowing him he would soon suspect the motive which attracted me to his house, and this move, instead of furthering our plans, might produce great set-backs; but if you are really good-hearted and sympathetic enough not to let me die of sorrow from no longer receiving what I dare to demand of you, I will tell you of ways and means.'

At first I refused to hear them, and was soon weak enough to ask him about them. They consisted, sir, of seeing each other three times a week at the house of a Madame Berceil, a milliner in the Rue des Arcis, whose prudence and honesty Monsieur de . . . . guaranteed like those of his own mother.

'Since you are allowed to see your aunt who lives, you said, fairly near there, you must pretend to go and see this aunt, pay her short visits in fact, and come and spend the rest of the time that you would have given to her at the house of the woman I have told you about; if your aunt is asked questions she will reply that she does in fact receive you on the day when you say that you go to see her, it will therefore only be a question of measuring the length of the visits, and this is something you can be sure that nobody will take the trouble to do, from the moment they have confidence in you.'

I shall not tell you, sir, all the objections I made to Monsieur de .... in order to dissuade him from this project and to make him aware of the disadvantages; what would be the point of telling you about my resistance, since I succumbed in the end? I promised Monsieur de .... all that he asked me, twenty louis that he gave to Julie without my knowledge put this girl entirely in his power, and from then on I worked only towards my own ruin. In order to make it more complete, in order to intoxicate myself at more length and leisure with the sweet poison that was flowing into my heart, I pretended to confide in my aunt, I told her that a young woman friend (whom I had told the secret and who was to take responsibility for it) wanted to do me the kindness of taking me three times a week to her box at the Comédie Française, that I dared not tell my father for fear he opposed it, but that I would say I was coming to see her, and I begged her to corroborate this; after a little difficulty my aunt could no longer resist my pleas, we agreed that Julie would come in my place, and that after the play I would meet her there on the way back and return to the house with her. I embraced my aunt over and over again: with the fatal blindness of the passions I thanked her for being a party to my destruction, for opening the door to the errors that were to lead me to the edge of the tomb!

At last we began to meet at La Berceil's house; her shop was magnificent, her house very respectable, and she herself a woman of about forty in whom I thought one could have complete confidence. Alas, I had only too much both in her and in my lover ... the traitor, it is time to confess it, sir ... on the sixth occasion that I saw him in that fatal house, he acquired such a hold over me, he succeeded in seducing me to such a point that he took advantage of my weakness and I became in his arms the idol of his passion and the victim of my own. . . . Cruel pleasures, what tears you have already cost me, and with what remorse you will rend my soul until the very last moment of my life!

A year passed in this state of fatal illusion, sir, I had just attained my seventeenth year; my father spoke to me every day about a marriage settlement, and you can imagine how I used to tremble at these propositions, when a fatal adventure at last hurled me into the everlasting abyss into which I had plunged. It was a gloomy dispensation of providence, no doubt, which arranged for something in which I had done no wrong to bring punishment for my genuine faults, to show that we can never escape from it, that it pursues everywhere anyone who strays, and that it is the incident we suspect the least which leads impercept-ibly to the one which is to serve its revenge.

Monsieur de .... had warned me one day that some business matter would inescapably deprive him of the pleasure of seeing me for the three whole hours we usually spent together; he would, however, come for a few minutes before the end of our rendezvous, while in order not to disturb our usual arrangements I should come to La Berceil's house for the time I normally spent there, and in fact for an hour or two I would find more entertainment with this milliner and her girls than I would all alone with my father; I believed I could rely on this woman sufficiently to find no obstacle to my lover's suggestion; I promised therefore that I would come and begged him not to be too late. He assured me that he would free himself as soon as possible, and I arrived; what a terrible day that was for me!

La Berceil received me at the entrance to her shop, without allowing me to go up to her own apartment as she usually did.

'Mademoiselle,' she said to me as soon as she saw me, 'I am delighted that Monsieur de .... cannot come here early this evening, I have something to confide to you that I dare not tell him, something which means that we must both go out quickly for a few moments, which we could not have done if he had been here.'

'What is the matter then, madame?' I said, somewhat alarmed by this beginning.

'Nothing much, mademoiselle, nothing,' La Berceil went on, 'calm yourself for a start, it is the simplest thing in the world; my mother has noticed your intrigue, she is an old shrew as fussy as a confessor whom I handle carefully because of her money. She is determined that I should not receive you any longer, I dare not tell Monsieur de . . . ., but this is what I have thought out. I am going to take you at once to one of my friends, a woman of my age and as reliable as I am, I will introduce you to her; if you like her, you will tell Monsieur de . . . . that I took you there, that she is a respectable woman and that you are quite happy for your meetings to take place in her house; if you do not like her, which is most unlikely, you will conceal our action from him, since we will only have been there for a moment, I will then take it upon myself to tell him that I can no longer lend him my house and you will consult together in order to find other ways of seeing each other.'

What this woman said was so simple, the air and the tone she used so natural, my confidence so complete and my innocence so perfect that I found no difficulty at all in agreeing to what she asked; I was only sorry about the fact that it was impossible, she alleged, for her to continue rendering services to us, I told her so wholeheartedly, and we went out. The house where I was being taken was in the same street, sixty or eighty paces away at the most from that of La Berceil; nothing displeased me from the outside, there was a carriage entrance, handsome windows looking on to the street, an air of decency and cleanliness all round; and yet a secret voice seemed to cry out in the depths of my heart that some strange happening awaited me in this fatal house; I felt a kind of repugnance at each step I mounted, everything seemed to say to me: 'Where are you going, unhappy girl, leave this treacherous place. . . ."
We arrived however, we entered a fairly fine antechamber where we found nobody and from there we went into a

drawing-room, the door closed behind us at once, as though someone were hiding behind it. . . . I shuddered, it was very dark in this drawing-room, we could barely see to walk across it; we had not taken more than three paces when I felt myself seized by two women, then the door of a small room opened and I saw inside it a man of about fifty along with two other women who called out to those who had grabbed hold of me: 'Undress her, undress her and don't bring her here until she's completely naked.'

I recovered from the shock I had felt when the women had laid hands on me, and seeing that my salvation depended more on my shouts than on my fears, I uttered terrifying cries. La Berceil did all she could to calm me.

'It only takes a moment, mademoiselle,' she said, 'just be a little accommodating, I beg you, and you will earn me fifty louis.'

'Disgusting shrew,' I cried, 'don't imagine that you can traffic in my honour, I shall throw myself out of the window if you do not let me out of here at once.'

'You would only fall into a courtyard of ours from where you would soon be recaptured, my child,' said one of the wretched women, while tearing off my clothes, 'so believe me, the quickest way is to let them do as they wish. . . .'

Oh, sir, spare me the rest of these horrible details, I was made naked in a moment, my cries were stifled by barbarous methods, and I was dragged towards the unworthy man, who, making light of my tears and laughing at my resistance, concerned himself only with the wretched victim whose heart he was breaking; two women held me continually and delivered me to this monster, and, although he was in a position to do anything he wished, he only satisfied his guilty ardour through impure caresses and kisses which did not outrage me. . . .

I was quickly helped to dress and placed in the hands of La Berceil again, in a state of collapse and confusion, gripped by a dark and bitter grief which froze my tears in the depths of my heart; I looked at the woman with fury. . . .

'Mademoiselle,' she said in terrible agitation, while still in the anteroom of this fateful house, 'I realise all the horror

of what I have just done, but I beg you to forgive me . . .
and at least to think things over before deciding to cause a
scandal; if you reveal this to Monsieur de . . . . , it is all very
well to say that you were forced into it, it is a kind of fault
that he will never forgive you, and you will quarrel for ever
with the one man in the world whom it is most important
for you to handle carefully, since you have no other means
of repairing the honour of which he has robbed you except
by making him agree to marry you. And you can be sure
that he will never do so if you tell him what has just
happened.'

'Wretched woman, why did you hurl me into this abyss,
why did you put me in such a situation that I have to
deceive my lover or else lose both my honour and him as
well?'

'Be calm, mademoiselle, let us speak no more of what
has happened, time passes, let us concern ourselves only
with what must be done. If you speak, you are lost; if you
say nothing, my house will always be open to you, you will
never be betrayed by anyone whatsoever, and you will stay
with your lover; revenge would bring you small satisfaction and in reality means nothing to me because,
knowing your secret, I can quite easily prevent Monsieur
de . . . . from harming me; see if the small pleasure of this
revenge can compensate you for all the sorrow it will
bring. . . .'

I realised then what a dishonourable woman I was
dealing with, and became aware of the force of her reasoning, however terrible it was.

'Let us go, madame, let us go,' I said to her, 'do not leave
me here any longer, I shall not say a word, you do the same;
I shall make use of you, since I could not break with you
without revealing disgraceful things that it is essential for
me to conceal, but at least I shall have the satisfaction in
the depths of my heart of hating you and despising you as
much as you deserve to be.'

We returned to La Berceil's house. . . . Gracious heaven,
what new anxiety seized me when we were told that
Monsieur de . . . . had been there, that he had been informed

that Madame had gone out on urgent business and that Mademoiselle had not yet come, while at the same time one of the girls in the house gave me a note that he had written for me in haste. It contained only these words: 'I do not find you, I imagine that you have not been able to come at the usual time, I cannot see you this evening, it is impossible for me to wait, I will see you the day after tomorrow without fail.'

This note in no way calmed me, its coldness seemed to me a bad sign . . . all this disturbed me to an indescribable extent; could he not have seen us go out, and followed us, and if he had done this, was I not lost? La Berceil, who was as anxious as I was, questioned everyone, she was told that Monsieur de . . . . had come three minutes after we had left, that he appeared very anxious, that he had gone out again at once and had returned to write this note, about half an hour afterwards. More anxious still, I sent for a carriage . . . but would you believe, sir, to what degree of effrontery that dishonourable woman dared to carry vice?

'Mademoiselle,' she told me as she saw me leaving, 'never say a word about this, I certainly recommend you not to, but if unfortunately you should break with Monsieur de . . . . believe me, take advantage of your liberty to make assignments, it is much more worthwhile than having a lover; I know you are a respectable young girl, but you are young, you are certainly given very little money, and since you are so pretty I could earn you as much as you want. Go on now, you're not the only one, there are girls like this who become very grand, who marry, as you will be able to one day, counts and marquesses, and who, either of their own accord, or through their governesses, have passed through our hands like you; we have men who are just right for nice little girls like you, you've seen it for yourself, they pluck you like a rose, they breathe you in and don't bruise you; farewell, my pretty, let us not be unpleasant to each other in any case, you can see clearly that I can still be useful to you.'

I looked at this creature with horror and left at once

without replying; I met Julie again at my aunt's house, as I always did, and returned home.

I no longer had any means of sending a message to Monsieur de .... for when we saw each other three times a week we were not in the habit of writing to each other, therefore I had to wait for the rendezvous. . . . What would he say to me? . . . what would I reply? Should I conceal what had happened, was there not the greatest danger that the truth might leak out, was it not much wiser to tell him everything? . . . All these different possibilities kept me in a state of indescribable anxiety. At last I determined to follow La Berceil's advice and, feeling quite certain that this woman was the most likely to benefit from secrecy, I decided to follow her example and say nothing. . . . Good heavens, what was the use of all these schemes, since I was not to see my lover again and the storm which was about to break over my head was already muttering on all sides!

The day after this incident my elder brother asked me why I allowed myself to go out as I did several times a week and at such hours.

'I go to spend the evening with my aunt,' I told him.

'That is false, Emilie, you have not set foot there for a month.'

'Well, my dear brother,' I replied, trembling, 'I shall tell you everything: one of my friends whom you know well, Madame de Saint-Clair, is kind enough to take me three times a week to her box at the Comédie Française, I did not dare to say anything about it, for fear my father disapproved, but my aunt knows all about it.'

'So you go to the play,' said my brother, 'you could have told me, I would have accompanied you, and the procedure would have been simple . . . but going alone with a woman who is no relative of yours and almost as young as you are . . .'

'Come, come, my friend,' said my other brother, who had joined us during this conversation, 'mademoiselle has her diversions, we mustn't disturb them . . . she's looking for a husband, they'll certainly appear in droves if she behaves like this. . . .'

And they both turned their backs on me coldly. This conversation frightened me; and yet my elder brother appeared reasonably convinced by my story about going to the theatre, I thought I had succeeded in deceiving him and that he would stop at that; besides, if either of them had said anything more, short of being locked in, nothing in the world would have stopped me from going to the next rendezvous; it had become too essential for me to have an explanation with my lover for anything whatever to deprive me of going to see him.

As for my father, he was still the same, idolising me, suspecting nothing of my faults, and never restricting me in any way. How cruel it is to have to deceive such parents, and how the remorse which follows brings thorns to the pleasures one buys at the expense of such treachery! Fatal example, cruel passion, may you preserve from my errors those who are in the same position as myself, and may the pains that these criminal pleasures have brought me halt them at least on the brink of the abyss, if ever they hear my deplorable story.

The fatal day arrived at last, I took Julie, and slipped out as usual, I left her at my aunt's and went at once in my fiacre to La Berceil's house. I got out . . . the silence and darkness which reigned in the house alarmed me greatly at first. . . . I saw no face I knew, there appeared only an old woman whom I had never seen and whom to my misfortune I was to see only too much! She told me to stay in the room where I was, that Monsieur de . . . . , she gave his name, was coming that moment to join me. I felt cold all over, and I collapsed into a chair without having the strength to say a word; I had hardly sat down when my two brothers appeared before me, with pistols in their hands.

'Wretched girl,' cried the elder, 'this is how you take us in; if you show the slightest resistance, if you utter a cry, you are dead. Follow us, we shall teach you if you can deceive both the family whom you are dishonouring and the lover to whom you used to give yourself.'

At these last words I lost consciousness completely and

only recovered it to find myself in the back of a carriage which seemed to me to be going very fast, between my two brothers and the old woman whom I mentioned, my legs tied together and my two hands bound with a hand-kerchief; the tears which so far had been kept back by my excessive sorrow flowed abundantly and I spent an hour in a state which, however guilty I might have been, would have moved anyone except the two murderers who had me in their power. They did not speak to me all the way, I imitated their silence and immersed myself in my grief; we arrived finally the next day at eleven o'clock in the morning, between Coucy and Noyon, at a château situated in the depths of a wood, which belonged to my elder brother; the carriage entered the courtyard, I was ordered to stay there until the horses and the servants had been taken away; then my elder brother came for me.

'Follow me,' he said brutally, after he had released me ... I obeyed, trembling. . . . Heavens, how frightened I was, when I saw the horrifying place which was to serve as my retreat! It was a low, dark, and damp room, secured with iron bars and receiving a little daylight only through a window looking on to a wide ditch full of water.

'Here is your dwelling-place, mademoiselle,' my brothers told me, 'a daughter who dishonours her family deserves only this. . . . Your food will be in keeping with the rest of the treatment, this is what you will be given,' they went on, showing me a piece of bread like that given to animals, 'and since we do not want to make you suffer for long, while on the other hand we want to make it impossible for you to get out of here, these two women,' they said, showing me the old woman and another one not very different, 'whom we found at the château, will be ordered to bleed both your arms as many times a week as you used to meet Monsieur de .... at La Berceil's house; gradually, at least we hope so, this régime will lead you to the tomb and we shall only be really happy when we learn that the family is rid of the monster that you are.'

At these words they ordered the women to seize me, and in front of them the villains, sir, forgive me this expression, in front of them . . . the cruel men bled both my arms at once and did not stop this harsh treatment until they saw I had lost consciousness. When I came to myself I found them congratulating each other on their barbarous behaviour, and as though they wanted every blow to fall on me at once, as though they took pleasure in rending my heart at the same moment as they shed my blood, the elder took a letter out of his pocket and gave it to me: 'Read, mademoiselle,' he said to me, 'read, and learn to whom you owe your sufferings. . . .'

I opened it, trembling, my eyes could barely read those fatal characters, oh merciful God . . . it was my love himself, it was he who was betraying me; this is what his cruel letter said, its words are still engraved on my heart in characters of blood: 'I have been foolish enough to love your sister, sir, and rash enough to dishonour her; I was going to make good everything; consumed by remorse, I was going to fall at your father's feet, confess my guilt and ask him for his daughter's hand. I would have been certain of admitting my own guilt and I was ready to become one with you; just as I was forming these resolutions . . . my eyes, my own eyes convinced me that I was dealing with someone who was no more than a girl of the streets, who under cover of rendezvous directed by honourable and pure feelings, dared to go and satisfy the infamous desires of the most disgusting of men. Expect no reparations from me, sir, now, I no longer owe you anything, I no longer owe you anything expect abandonment, and to her the most inviolable hatred and the most utter scorn. I am sending you the address of the house where your sister used to go for this corrupt purpose, sir, so that you can verify if I am deceiving you.'

I had barely read these fatal words than I collapsed again in the most terrible state. . . . No, I said to myself, tearing my hair, no, cruel man, you never loved me: if the slightest feeling had ever touched your heart, would you have condemned me without hearing me, would you have supposed me guilty of such a crime when it was you whom I adored. . . . Traitor, and it is your hand that delivers me, it is you who are casting me into the hands of the murderers who will make me die a little each day . . . and die without being justified by you . . . to die despised by the only man I adore, when I have never voluntarily offended you, when I have only been duped and victimised, oh no, no, this situation is too cruel, it is beyond my strength to bear it! Throwing myself in tears at my brothers' feet I begged them either to listen or to stop shedding my blood drop by drop and to make me die at once.

They consented to listen to me, I told them my story, but they wanted to ruin me, and they did not believe me, they only treated me worse; after having finally overwhelmed me with invective, after having urged the two women to carry out their orders to the letter, under pain of death, they left me, assuring me coldly that they hoped never to see me again.

As soon as they had gone, my two warders left me bread and water and locked me in, but at least I was alone, I could abandon myself to the excesses of my sorrow, and I was less unhappy. The first feelings of my despair led me to unbandage my arms so that I might die through loss of blood. But the horrible idea of ceasing to live without vindicating myself before my lover rent me with such violence that I could never resolve to carry out this idea; a little calm restores hope . . . hope, this feeling of consolation which is always born in the midst of sorrow, divine gift bestowed on us by nature to compensate for it or to soften it. . . . No, I told myself, I shall not die without seeing him, I should work only for that, I should concern myself only with that; if he persists in believing me guilty, then it will be time to die and I shall at least do so without regret, since it is impossible for life to hold any attraction for me when I have lost his love.

Having made this decision, I resolved to neglect no means which could remove me from that hateful place. I had been consoling myself with this thought for four days when my two jailers reappeared to renew my provisions and at the same time to make me lose a little of the strength that they gave me; they bled me again in both arms and left me motionless on the bed; a week later they appeared again and since I threw myself at their feet in order to ask for mercy they only bled me in one arm. Two months passed in this way, during which I was continually bled alternately in each arm every four days. The strength of my constitution, the quantity of bread I ate in order to recover from my exhaustion and to be able to carry out my resolutions, everything went well for me, and towards the beginning of the third month I was fortunate enough to have pierced through a wall and to have passed through the hole I had made into a neighbouring room that was not locked. Finally I escaped from the château and I was trying as best I could to regain on foot the road to Paris, when my strength gave out completely at the place where you saw me and I obtained from you, sir, the generous help for which my sincere gratitude rewards you as much as possible; I dare to beg that you will maintain it towards me, in order to restore me to my father who has certainly been deceived and who will never be barbarous enough to condemn me without allowing me to prove my innocence to him. I shall convince him that I have been weak, but he will see clearly that I have not been as guilty as appearances would seem to prove; through this help, sir, you will not only have recalled to life an unfortunate creature who will never cease to thank you for it, but you will also have restored honour to a family who believe that they have been unjustly deprived of it.

'Mademoiselle,' said the Comte de Luxeuil, after having given all possible attention to Emilie's story, 'it is difficult to see you and listen to you without taking the most lively interest in you: no doubt you have not been as guilty as one might believe, but there is a certain rashness about your conduct which must be very difficult for you to conceal from yourself.'

'Oh, sir!'

'Listen, mademoiselle, I beg you, listen to the man who is more anxious than anyone in the world to help you. Your lover's conduct has been terrible, not only was it unjust, for he should have informed himself better and seen you, but it was even cruel; if one is prejudiced to the point of no return, one abandons a woman in that case, but one does not denounce her to her family, one does not dishonour her, one does not hand her over unworthily to those who want to ruin her, one does not urge them to avenge themselves. . . . I criticise greatly therefore the conduct of the man you loved . . . but that of your brothers is even more unworthy, it is atrocious from all points of view, only murderers can behave like this. Faults of this kind do not deserve such punishment; restraints have never served any useful purpose; one remains silent in such cases but one neither sheds the blood of the guilty party nor removes his liberty; these odious methods bring much more dishonour to those who employ them than to those who are the victims of them, they have deserved their hate, they have caused a good deal of scandal and have set nothing right. However much we prize a sister's honour her life should have a very different value in our eyes, honour can be restored, but not blood that has been shed; this conduct is therefore so horrible that it would certainly be punished if one lodged a complaint with the government, but methods which would only imitate those of your persecutors, which would only noise abroad the things we should suppress are not those we must use. I shall therefore act in a completely different way in order to serve you, mademoiselle, but I warn you that I can only do so under the following conditions: the first is that you should write down for me the exact addresses of your father, your aunt, La Berceil, and of the man to whom La Berceil took you, while the second, mademoiselle, is that you name me without any hindrance the man who interests you. This condition is absolutely essential and I do not conceal from you that it is totally impossible for me to serve you in any way whatsoever if you persist in keeping from me the name I demand.'

Emilie was confused and began by fulfilling the first condition exactly, giving the addresses to the Comte.

'So you are demanding me, sir,' she said with a blush, 'to give you the name of my seducer. . . .'

'Precisely, mademoiselle, I can do nothing without it.'

'Well, sir, it was the Marquis de Luxeuil . . .'

'The Marquis de Luxeuil!' cried the Comte, unable to disguise the emotion with which the name of his son filled him . . . to think that he was capable of such a thing . . . he . . . Then he pulled himself together: 'He will make it good, mademoiselle . . . he will make it good and you will be avenged . . . you have my word for it, farewell.'

The amazing agitation into which Emilie's last confidence had thrown the Comte de Luxeuil surprised the unfortunate girl greatly, she feared she had committed an indiscretion; however she was reassured by the Comte's words as he went out, and without understanding anything of the connection between these inextricable facts, not knowing where she was, she decided to wait patiently the result of her benefactor's actions, and the care that was still taken of her while these went on finally calmed her and convinced her that everything was being done in the interests of her happiness.

She had every reason to be entirely convinced of this when, four days after the explanations that she had given, she saw the Comte enter the room leading the Marquis de Luxeuil by the hand.

'Mademoiselle,' said the Comte, 'I am bringing you both the cause of your misfortunes and the man who is coming to make them good to you, begging you on his knees not to refuse him your hand.'

At these words the Marquis threw himself at the feet of the girl he adored, but this surprise had been too great for Emilie; she was not strong enough to bear it and fainted in the arms of the woman who was looking after her; after care however she quickly recovered her senses again in the arms of her lover.

'Cruel man,' she said to him, weeping copiously, 'what sorrows you have caused the girl you love! Could you believe her capable of the infamous conduct of which you have dared to suspect her? In loving you Emilie could be the victim of her weakness and the trickery of others, but she could never be unfaithful to you.'

'Oh you whom I adore,' cried the Marquis, 'forgive the transport of horrible jealousy based on deceptive impressions, we are now all quite sure about it, but did these impressions not tell against you in a fatal manner, alas?'

'You should have valued me, Luxeuil, and you would not have believed that I was capable of deceiving you, you should have heeded not so much your despair as the feelings which I flattered myself I inspired in you. May this example teach my sex that it is nearly always through too much love . . . almost always in yielding too quickly that we lose the esteem of our lovers. . . . Oh, Luxeuil, you could have loved me better if I had loved you less quickly, you have punished me for my weakness, and your love should be strengthened by the feelings which made you suspect mine.'

'May all be forgotten on all sides,' interrupted the Comte; 'Luxeuil, your conduct was to be blamed and if you had not offered to set it right immediately, if I had not known that in your heart you wanted to, I would never have seen you again for the rest of my life. *When one truly loves,* our ancient troubadours used to say, *if one hears or sees something to the detriment of one's mistress, one should believe neither one's ears nor one's eyes, one must listen only to one's heart.** Mademoiselle, I await your recovery with impatience,' went on the Comte, addressing Emilie, 'I wish to take you back to your parents only as my son's wife and I flatter myself that they will not refuse to ally themselves with me in order to make good your misfortunes; if they do not do so, I offer you my house, mademoiselle; your marriage will be celebrated there, and until my dying breath I shall not cease to see you as a cherished daughter-in-law by whom I shall always be honoured, whether her marriage is approved or not.'

The Marquis threw himself into his father's arms, Mademoiselle de Tourville dissolved into tears while seizing her benefactor's hands, and she was left for several hours to

* It is the Provençal troubadours who said this, not those of Picardy.

recover from a scene which, if it had lasted too long, would have had an adverse effect on the convalescence which was so ardently desired on all sides.

Two weeks in fact after her return to Paris, Mademoiselle de Tourville was fit to get up and enter a carriage, the Comte had her clothed in a white dress in keeping with the innocence of her heart, nothing was neglected in order to enhance her charms which a slight pallor and weakness rendered even more attractive; the Comte, she and the Marquis went to the Président de Tourville, who had been informed of nothing and was extremely surprised to see his daughter enter. He was with his two sons, whose faces became angry and enraged at this unexpected sight; they knew that their sister had escaped but they believed her dead in some corner of the forest and had consoled themselves for the fact without the slightest difficulty.

'Monsieur,' said the Comte, presenting Emilie to her father, 'I am bringing back innocence itself to kneel before you,' and Emilie rushed forward . . .

'I beg forgiveness on her behalf, sir,' the Comte went on, 'and I would not ask you for it if I were not certain that she deserves it; moreover, sir,' he went on rapidly, 'the best proof I can give you of the high esteem I have for your daughter is that I ask her hand in marriage on behalf of my son. Our ranks are suitable for alliance sir, and if something were lacking on my side as far as property were concerned, I would sell all I possessed to provide for my son a fortune worthy of being offered to your daughter. Make your decision, sir, and allow me not to leave you until I have your promise.'

The old Président de Tourville, who had always adored his dear Emilie, who in his heart of hearts was goodness personified, and who even because of the excellence of his character had not exercised his profession for more than twenty years, the old Président, I say, shedding tears over his beloved child, replied to the Comte that the only thing that upset him was that his dear Emilie was not worthy of it; and the Marquis de Luxeuil threw himself also on his knees in front of the Président, entreated him to forgive him his mistakes and to allow him to set them right. All the promises were made, everything was settled, everything grew calm on all sides, only our attractive heroine's brothers refused to share the general happiness and repulsed her when she went up to them to embrace them; the Comte was furious at such behaviour and wanted to stop one of them who was trying to leave the apartment. Monsieur de Tourville called out to the Comte:

'Leave them, sir, leave them, they have deceived me horribly; if this dear child had been as guilty as they told me, would you consent to give her to your son? They have troubled my happiness in depriving me of my Emilie . . . leave them alone. . . .' and the wretched men went out fulminating with rage.

Then the Comte told Monsieur de Tourville of all the horrible behaviour of his sons and the true errors of his daughter; the Président, seeing the lack of proportion there was between the errors and the indignity of the punishment, swore that he would never set eyes on his sons again; the Comte calmed him and made him promise that he would forget all that had happened. A week later the marriage was celebrated without the brothers wishing to attend it, but everyone dispensed with them and despised them, Monsieur de Tourville contented himself with urging them to maintain the most total silence under pain of putting them in prison themselves, and they remained silent, but not silent enough however to avoid priding themselves on their infamous behaviour by condemning their father's indulgence, and those who learnt of this unfortunate incident cried out, horrified by the atrocious details which characterised it: 'Oh gracious heavens, so these are the horrors silently permitted to themselves by those who want to punish the crimes of others!'

It is quite right to say that such infamous behaviour is reserved to those frenzied and clumsy supporters of Themis who, brought up in ridiculous severity, hardened from childhood to the cries of unhappiness, soiled with blood since the cradle, criticising everything and allowing themselves everything, imagine that the only way of concealing their secret shame and their public prevarications is to reveal a rigid severity which, likening them from the outside to geese, and from the inside to tigers, has no other object, in covering them with crime, than to impose on fools and to make wise men detest their hateful principles, their sanguinary laws and their despicable personalities.

ROOM FOR TWO

A VERY ATTRACTIVE TOWNSWOMAN who lived in the Rue St. Honoré, aged about twenty-two, plump and chubby, whose body was extremely fresh and appetising, well-formed although somewhat full in its contours, and who possessed in addition to so many charms a present wit, vivacity, and the most lively taste for all the pleasures forbidden to her by the strict rules of marriage, had decided about a year earlier to find two assistants for her husband who, being old and ugly, not only displeased her a great deal, but even carried out his duties both badly and rarely while if he had fulfilled them a little better he might perhaps have satisfied the demanding Dolmène, as our delightful townswoman was called.

Nothing was better arranged than the appointments made with these two lovers: Des-Roues, a young military man, usually had from four to five in the afternoon, and between half-past five and seven came Dolbreuse, a young businessman with the most attractive appearance imaginable. It was impossible to fix other times, these were the only ones when Madame Dolmène was undisturbed: in the morning she had to go to the shop, sometimes she had to go there in the evening too, or else her husband came back and she had to talk about business. Moreover Madame Dolmène had confided to one of her women friends that she rather liked these moments of pleasure to follow one another in quick succession: in this way the fires of imagination did not die down, she maintained, there was nothing so delightful as to go from one pleasure to another, one did not have the trouble of getting under way again; for Madame Dolmène was a charming creature who calculated to the best advantage all the sensations of love, very few women analysed them as she did and thanks to her talents she had recognised that, when all was said and done, two lovers were much better than one; as far as reputation went things were more or less the same, one protected the other, people could be mistaken, it could be always the same man who came and went several times during the day, and as far as pleasure was concerned, what a difference it made! Madame Dolmène was exceptionally afraid of pregnancy, and, feeling certain that her husband would never commit the folly of spoiling her figure, had also calculated that with two lovers there was much less risk of what she feared than with one, for, as she used to say, speaking as a reasonably good anatomist, the two fruits of love would mutually destroy one another.

One particular day the order of the appointments happened to be upset, and the two lovers, who had never seen each other, became acquainted, as we shall see, in a somewhat amusing fashion. Des-Roues was first, but he had come too late, and as though the devil had intervened, Dolbreuse, who was second, arrived somewhat too early.

The intelligent reader will see at once that these two little mistakes would unfortunately lead to an inevitable encounter: which therefore took place. But let us describe how this occurred and, if we can, let us tell of it with all the decency and restraint demanded by such events which are already very licentious in themselves.

Through a rather strange caprice—but one sees so many of them among mankind—our young soldier was weary of playing the lover and for a moment wanted to play that of mistress; instead of being amorously held in the arms of his goddess he wanted to hold her in his turn: in other words he placed upwards what is usually underneath, and through this reversal of roles it was Madame Dolmène, leaning over the altar where the sacrifice is usually performed, naked as Venus Callipygus, who presented, facing the door to the bedroom where the rites were being celebrated, that part of the body which the Greeks worshipped with devotion in the statue to which we have just referred, this part which in fact is so beautiful, and without seeking examples so far afield, finds so many admirers in Paris. Such was her position when Dolbreuse, accustomed to enter the house freely, arrived humming a tune, and his eyes fell upon that which, according to tradition, a truly honest woman should never show.

The sight which would have greatly pleased many people caused Dolbreuse to draw back.

'What do I see?' he cried . . . 'traitress . . is this the place you reserve for me?'

Madame Dolmène was at that moment passing through one of those crises in which a woman acts infinitely better than she reasons, and she decided to be equally audacious in return:

'What the devil's the matter with you?' she said to the second Adonis, without ceasing to give herself to the other, 'I can't see anything particularly upsetting from your point of view; don't disturb us, my friend, and take your place in what's left to you; you can easily see there's room for two.'

Dolbreuse couldn't help laughing at his mistress' sang-froid and, believing that the simplest thing was to follow her advice, did not wait to be asked again, and apparently all three of them enjoyed themselves more this way.

THE SELF-MADE
CUCKOLD
or The Unexpected Reconciliation

ONE OF THE GREATEST defects in ill-bred persons is that
they constantly risk a host of indiscretions, untruths or
calumnies about everyone living, and that in front of people
they do not know; one cannot imagine the number of
problems caused by chatter of this sort: what honest man
can in fact hear evil spoken of someone who interests him
without reprimanding the fool who risks the remark? This
principle of prudent reticence is not introduced into the
education of young people often enough, they are not
adequately taught to know society, the names, qualities
and attributes of the people with whom they are accustomed to live; instead they are taught countless silly things
which are only fit to be discarded once the age of reason is
reached. One has the impression that everyone is being
brought up like Capuchins: bigotry, mummery or futilities
all the time, and never a sound moral maxim. Go further,
ask a young man about his real duties towards society, ask
him what are his duties towards himself and others, how he
should conduct himself in order to be happy: he will tell
you that he has been taught to go to Mass and recite

litanies, but that he understands nothing of what you are trying to tell him, that he has been taught how to dance and sing but not how to live with men. The developments which followed the unfortunate incident that we are describing were not serious enough to lead to bloodshed, they led only to a joke, and we are going to abuse our readers' patience for a few moments in order to recount it.

Monsieur de Raneville, who was about fifty, was one of those phlegmatic characters whom one does not meet in society without a certain pleasure: he laughed little, but through making others laugh a good deal, through the sallies of his mordant wit and the cool manner in which he uttered them he often found, either through merely remaining silent, or through the comical expression on his taciturn face, the secret of amusing the circles he frequented a thousand times more than those heavy-going, monotonous chatterers who have always a story to tell you over which they laugh an hour in advance, but the stories are never good enough to amuse the listeners for a moment. He possessed a fairly large income as a tax-farmer and in order to console himself for a very unsatisfactory marriage which he had contracted earlier in Orleans, he had deserted his dishonest wife there, and was now calmly spending twenty or twenty-five thousand livres of unearned income in Paris with a very pretty woman whom he maintained and a few friends as likeable as himself.

Monsieur de Raneville's mistress was not exactly a prostitute, she was a married woman and consequently more piquant, for in spite of all one can say this touch of adulterous spice often increases enjoyment greatly; she was extremely pretty, aged about thirty, with the finest figure in the world; separated from a dull and boring husband, she had come from the provinces to seek her fortune in Paris, and had not taken long to make it. Raneville, who was a natural libertine with an eye open for every tempting morsel, had not let this one escape, and for three years, through very honourable treatment, much wit and much money, he had caused this young woman to forget all the sorrows which marriage had brought her in the past. Since both of them had more or less the same fate, they consoled each other together and confirmed this great truth—which however reforms nobody—that there are only so many unhappy marriages, and, as a result, so much unhappiness in the world, because miserly or stupid parents marry off fortunes rather than temperaments: for, as Raneville often said to his mistress, 'it is indeed certain that if fate had united us, instead of giving you a tyrannical and ridiculous husband and me a whore for a wife, roses would have grown in our path rather than the thorns we have gathered for so long.'

An incident of no particular importance led Monsieur de Raneville one day to that muddy and unhealthy village called Versailles, where kings made to be adored in their capital seem to flee the presence of subjects who want them, where ambition, avarice, revenge and pride daily bring together a host of unfortunates going on the wings of boredom to sacrifice to the idol of the day, where the elite of French nobility, which could play an important part in their country estates, consent to humiliate themselves in antechambers, pay court in a servile fashion to Swiss guards, or humbly beg a dinner inferior to the meal they eat at home from some of those individuals whom fortune snatches from the clouds of forgetfulness for a moment before plunging them back there shortly afterwards.

After concluding his business Monsieur de Raneville entered one of those court carriages known as a *pot de chambre* and by chance found himself seated next to a certain Monsieur Dutour, very talkative, very rotund, very fat and given to much laughter, employed like Monsieur de Raneville in tax-farming, but hailing from Orleans, which as we know was also Monsieur de Raneville's home town. They got into conversation and Raneville, continually laconic and revealing nothing, already knew the name, surname, place or origin and the business of his travelling companion, without saying a single word himself. Once these details had been supplied Monsieur Dutour entered rather more into those concerning society.

'You have been to Orleans, sir,' said Dutour, 'I think that you just told me so.'

'I stayed there for a few months in the past.'

'I wonder if you met Madame de Raneville, one of the greatest prostitutes who ever lived in Orleans?'

'Madame de Raneville, a somewhat pretty woman?'

'Precisely.'

'Yes, I came across her in society.'

'Well, I will tell you confidently that I had her, that is to say for three days, the way one has that sort of thing. Indeed if ever there was a deceived husband, the unfortunate Raneville is certainly one of them.'

'And do you know him?'

'No, he's a bad type who's ruining himself in Paris, they say, with whores and libertines like himself.'

'I can't tell you anything about him, I don't know him, but I pity deceived husbands; you're not one yourself, sir, by chance?'

'Which of the two do you mean, sir, a husband or a deceived one?'

'Both in fact, the two are so closely linked today that it's very difficult in fact to tell the difference between them.'

'I am married, sir, and I had the misfortune to marry a woman who could not settle down with me; since her character was also very unsuitable for me, we separated on good terms, she wanted to come to Paris to share the solitude of one of her relatives, who is a nun at the convent of St. Aure, and she lives there, sending me news of herself from time to time, but I never see her.'

'Is she religious?'

'No, I might perhaps like her better if she were.'

'Ah, I understand you. And have you not even had the curiosity to enquire about her health, during the stay which business forces you to make in Paris at the moment?'

'No, for in fact I don't like convents: I like pleasure and gaiety, I was made for enjoyment, I'm sought after in society, I don't want to risk having the vapours for six months through going into a convent parlour.'

'But a wife . . .'

'. . . is an individual who can be interesting when one makes use of her, but one must know how to detach oneself firmly when serious reasons separate one from her.'

'That is a harsh statement.'

'Not at all . . . it is philosophy . . . it is the tone of the day, it is the language of reason, one must adopt it or be taken for a fool.'

'This supposes some fault in your wife, explain it to me: some natural defect, or a failure to comply, or bad conduct.'

'A little of everything . . . a little of everything, sir, but let us change the subject, I beg you, and return to that dear Madame de Raneville: damn me, I don't understand how you can have been in Orleans without amusing yourself with that creature . . . but everyone has her.'

'Not everyone, for you can see that I haven't had her: I don't like married women.'

'And without being too inquisitive, how do you pass your time, sir, I beg you?'

'In business at first, and then with a pretty creature with whom I take supper from time to time.'

'You are not married, sir?'

'I am.'

'And your wife?'

'She is in the provinces and I leave her there, as you leave yours at St. Aure.'

'You are married, sir, married, and if you belong to the brotherhood I beg you to tell me.'

'Did I not tell you that husband and cuckold are synonymous terms?'

'Depraved morals, luxury . . . so many things cause a woman's downfall.'

'Oh, it's very true, sir, it's very true.'

'You answer like a man who knows.'

'No, not at all; so, sir, a pretty woman consoles you for the absence of your deserted wife.'

'Yes, indeed, a very pretty woman, I should like you to make her acquaintance.'

'Sir, you do me great honour.'

'Oh, not at all, sir, now we are arriving, I will leave you free this evening because of your business, but tomorrow I shall expect you without fail for supper at this address,' and Raneville carefully gave a false one, of which he informed those at his house so that anyone who came to ask for him under the name he gave could find him easily.

The next day Monsieur Dutour did not fail to come at the appointed time, and precautions having been taken so that he could find Raneville in the house even under an assumed name, he entered without difficulty. After the first compliments had been exchanged, Dutour seemed upset at not seeing the goddess on whom he was counting.

'Impatient man,' Raneville said to him, 'I can see from here what you are looking for . . . you have been promised a pretty woman, you want to flutter round her; since you are accustomed to dishonour the husbands of Orleans you want, I am sure, to treat the lovers of Paris in the same way! I wager that you would gladly put me in the same boat as that unfortunate Raneville whom you described to me so amusingly yesterday.'

Dutour replied like a Don Juan, a vain and consequently a foolish man, the conversation brightened for a moment and then Raneville took his friend by the hand.

'Come,' he said, 'you cruel man, come into the very temple where the goddess is awaiting you.'

So saying he took Dutour into a small voluptuous room, where Raneville's mistress, who had been told of the joke and was in the secret, was lying on a velvet-covered sofa, clad in the most elegant déshabillé, but veiled: nothing concealed the elegant curves of her figure, only her face was invisible.

'There is a very beautiful woman,' cried Dutour, 'but why do you deprive me of the pleasure of admiring her features, are we in the great lord's seraglio?'

'No, not a word, it is a question of modesty.'

'What do you mean, modesty?'

'Do you think I want to restrict myself to showing you only my mistress' figure or dress? Would my triumph be complete if, in removing all these veils, I did not convince you how happy I ought to be in possessing so many charms . . . ? Since this young woman is remarkably modest, she would blush at these details; she was prepared to agree to this, but on the express condition of being veiled. You know what women's modesty and delicacy are like, Monsieur Dutour, one doesn't deceive an elegant and fashionable man like you over these things. . . .'

'What, are you really going to show me . . . ?'

'Everything, I told you so, nobody is less jealous than I am, happiness that one enjoys alone appears insipid to me, I only find enjoyment when it is shared.'

And in order to prove his statements Raneville began by removing a gauze kerchief which immediately revealed the most beautiful bosom that could possibly be seen. . . . Dutour became excited.

'Well,' said Raneville, 'what do you think of that?'

'As attractive as Venus herself.'

'Do you think that breasts so white and firm are made to arouse passions . . . ? touch them, touch them, my friend, eyes can sometimes deceive us, I believe that in pleasure all the senses should be employed.'

Dutour came close with a trembling hand, felt with ecstasy the most beautiful breast in the world and could not get over his friend's unbelievable complaisance.

'Let us go a little further down,' said Raneville, raising a skirt of light taffeta up to the waist, and meeting no opposition to this move. 'Well, what have you to say about these thighs, can you believe that the temple of love is supported by columns more beautiful?'

The dear Dutour continued to squeeze everything Raneville revealed.

'Rogue, I guess how you feel,' the complaisant friend went on, 'this delicate temple which the Graces themselves have covered with a light moss . . . you're burning to open it, aren't you? What am I saying, to kiss it, I wager.'

And Dutour was blinded . . . he stammered . . . he replied only through the violence of the sensations recorded by his eyes; his friend urged him on . . . his libertine fingers caressed the doors of the temple which voluptuousness itself opened to his desires; he gave the divine kiss that was permitted and savoured it for an hour.

'My friend,' he said, ' I can bear it no longer, either drive me out of your house or allow me to go further.'

'What the devil, further, and how far do you want to go, I beg you?'

'Alas, don't you understand me, I'm intoxicated with love, I can contain myself no longer.'

'And what if this woman is ugly?'

'It is impossible to be ugly with such divine charms.'

'If she is. . . .'

'She can be as ugly as she pleases, I tell you, my friend, I can resist her no longer.'

'Go on then, my fierce friend, go on then, satisfy yourself since you must: you will at least be grateful for my co-operation?'

'Oh, as much as possible, certainly.'

And Dutour pushed his friend gently away as though to make him leave him alone with this woman.

'Oh, as for leaving you, no I can't,' said Raneville, 'but are you so scrupulous then that you cannot satisfy yourself in my presence? Between men we don't worry about that sort of thing: moreover, those are my conditions, either in front of me or not at all.'

'If it was in front of the devil,' said Dutour, containing himself no longer, and rushing to the sanctuary where his incense was to be burnt, 'you wish it, I agree to everything. . . .'

'Well,' said Raneville phlegmatically, 'have appearances deceived you and are the delights promised by so many charms illusory or real? Ah, never, never did I see anything so voluptuous.'

'But this damnable veil, my friend, this treacherous veil, will I not be allowed to remove it?'

'Yes, at the last moment, at that moment so delectable when all our senses are seduced by the intoxication of the gods, and she knows how to make us as happy as they are, and often even more so. This surprise will double your ecstasy; to the delight of enjoying the body of Venus herself you will add the inexpressible pleasure of contemplating the features of Flora, and as everything combines to increase your happiness, you will plunge much more deeply into that ocean of pleasures in which men find with so much delight the consolation of their existence. . . . You will make a sign to me. . . .'

'Oh, you will see when it is,' said Dutour. 'I am carried away at that moment.'

'Yes, I see, you are impassioned.'

'But impassioned to a point . . . oh, my friend, I have reached that celestial moment, tear off these veils, tear them off, let me look on heaven itself.'

'There it is,' said Raneville, drawing back the gauze, 'but take care lest this paradise be not far from hell!'

'Good God,' cried Dutour, recognising his wife . . . 'it's you, madame . . . sir, what a strange joke, you deserve . . . this wretched woman . . .'

'One moment, one moment, impassioned man, it is you who deserve everything; learn, my friend, that one must be a little more circumspect with people whom one does not know than you were yesterday with me. The unfortunate Raneville, whom you treated so badly at Orleans . . . I am he, sir; you can see that I am paying you back in Paris; moreover, you are much more advanced than you thought, you believed that I was the only cuckold you had made, and you have just made yourself one all on your own.'

Dutour understood the lesson, he held out his hand to his friend and agreed that he had had his deserts.

'But this treacherous woman . . .'

'Well, is she not following your example? What is the barbarous law which enslaves this sex in an inhuman fashion while giving us all the liberty we want? Is it equitable? And by what natural right do you lock up your wife in St. Aure while cuckolding husbands in Paris and Orleans?'

'My friend, that is not correct, the charming creature whom you did not know how to value came to make other conquests; she was right, she found me; I bring her happiness, you must do the same for Madame Raneville, I permit it, let us all four live happily together, and may the victims of fate not become the victims of men.'

Dutour found that his friend was right, but through an inconceivable fatality, he fell madly in love again with his wife; Raneville, in spite of his caustic tongue, was too high-minded to resist Dutour's pleas to have his wife back again, the young woman agreed to it, and this unique incident is no doubt a most strange example of the blows of fate and the capriciousness of love.

Also published by Peter Owen

THE MARQUIS de SADE READER:
The Passionate Philosopher
Edited and translated by Margaret Crosland

0 7206 1090 7 • Paperback • 183pp • £12.95

For all his notoriety, the Marquis de Sade must head the list of writers who are more talked about than read, but in this representative selection Margaret Crosland encourages us to take a fresh look at his work. Sade spent more than half his life in prison and, excluded from normal life, he developed an extremist vision of the world through stories, dialogues and historical novels. Included here are extracts from his major fiction: some of the devastating fantasies in *Les Cent Vingt Journées de Sodome* as well as episodes from Justine and from the compulsively vicious Juliette.

Yet, in addition to his so-called 'obscene' writing, Sade wrote with equal fervour about idealized people and democratic societies. He was indeed a passionate philosopher, a man typical in many ways of his times but eager to pass on to later centuries his incandescent ideas about human behaviour.

Following her Introduction, Margaret Crosland provides astute commentaries on her selections and finally a Chronology and Bibliography.

'Beautifully produced . . . provides a detailed and comprehensive introduction to the work.' – *Gay Times*

Also published by Peter Owen

The Marquis de Sade

The Crimes of Love

0 7206 1183 0 • Paperback • 130pp • £9.95

'To brief stories of lewd monks, ruttish wives and cuckolds, he added longer and darker intrigues in the fashionable Gothic vein. Published as *Les Crimes de l'Amour*, they show off Sade's literary skills to good effect. They survive admirably in Margaret Crosland's excellent new translation of the five longer narratives.' – David Coward, *Times Literary Supplement*

The five stories in this extremely popular collection are taken from *Les Crimes de l'Amour*, originally published in 1800. They contrast with other writings by the Marquis, forming part of a significant genre of their own within the body of his work. In *The Crimes of Love* Sade contends that love can lead to crime and thence to punishment.

Unlike the villains of his major novels, the men and women described in these pages all come to a sticky end. Sade was fascinated by incest but claimed that he did 'not want to make vice liked'. The stories also illustrate his love of history and his frustrated passion for drama, while 'Rodrigo or the Enchanted Tower' is an intriguing example of this complex writer's flight into fantasy – his only means of escape from detention.

Translated from the French and with an introduction by Margaret Crosland

PETER OWEN MODERN CLASSICS

THE MISCREANT
JEAN COCTEAU
0 7206 1173 3 • Paperback • 172pp • £9.95

Jacques Forestier, the central character of Cocteau's famous first novel from 1921, is a parasite and dilettante who responds readily to to beauty in both sexes. Leaving his provincial family he comes to Paris to study for his degree. Indulging in a life of dissipation with a group of students and their mistresses, he falls in love with Germaine, a chorus girl kept by a rich banker. The affair, doomed from the start, forces Jacques to come to terms not so much with society as he finds it, but with himself.

Also containing line drawings by Cocteau, *The Miscreant* is a sparkling evocation of the Parisian scene of the 1920s.

'It is the book's universality that engages us: its persuasive account of Jacques's first love affair with the revue artiste Germaine, and his discovery that sexual behaviour is far too complex not to contradict the dreams of an adolescent . . . This adolescent world — recognizable and timeless — is so well realized the *The Miscreant* may seem unconnected with what was to come.'
— *Times Literary Supplement*

'Butterfly-like, brilliant, febrile . . . Cocteau's famous novel was all but a bible to avante-garde intellectuals of the 1920s.' — Elizabeth Bowen, *Tatler*

'Ultra-contemporary.' — *Time Out*

COLLAGES
ANAÏS NIN
0 7206 1145 8 • Paperback • 176pp • £9.95

Set in a world of fantasy and dreams, *Collages* dispenses with normal structural convention and allows its characters to wander freely in space and time in an attempt to describe life with the disconnected clarity of a dream.

Featuring characters from a gay Norwegian who keeps chapters of his past hidden inside Chinese boxes to a woman who provides witches' laughter on the radio and uses her dress as a tent, *Collages* is a series of impressions, a shifting notebook indelibly inscribed with Nin's humour, invention and unrivalled gift for sensuous description.

'A delight.' — *Independent*

'Nin uses words as magnificently colourful, evocative and imagist as any plastic combination on canvas but as mysteriously idiosyncratic as any abstract . . . Perfectly told fables and prose that is so daringly elaborate, so accurately timed that it is not entirely surprising to find her compared with Proust.' — *Times Literary Supplement*

'One of the most extraordinary and unconventional writers of the century.' — *New York Times*

PETER OWEN MODERN CLASSICS

TWO RIDERS OF THE STORM
JEAN GIONO
0 7206 1159 8 • Paperback • 240pp • £9.95

Two Riders of the Storm is set in the remote High Hill country of Provence where the lives of the inhabitants are moulded along fiercley passionate lines.

Two brothers, Marceau and Ange Jason are members of a family renowned and respected for its brutality and bound together with ties stronger than those of ordinary brotherly love. They spend their lives drinking, wresting, selling mules and driving the local women to force fodder from the harsh soil. But the bond must snap and the end, when it comes, is a violent – and deadly – confrontation.

Two Riders of the Storm is a story of a Cain-and-Abel-like struggle for supremacy described with an intense and stark poetic beauty that transforms its brutal imagery into elemental forces of life death.

'Giono gives us a world he lives in, a world of dream, passion and reality.'
– *Henry Miller*

'It has a timeless fairytale quality . . . The writing is zestful and broadly humorous, the philosophy that of a French D.H. Lawrence.' – *Sunday Times*

'Violent but beautiful . . . the explosive gusto of Giono's language marks him as a novelist of great originality.' – *Spectator*

RETREAT FROM LOVE
COLETTE
0 7206 1227 6 • Paperback • 232pp • £9.95

Retreat From Love is one of the best of Colette's celebrated 'Claudine' novels. A tale of the sexual and emotional machinations of three upper-class youths in a remote farmhouse, *Retreat From Love* shows the work of a newly mature Colette, a novelist now to be judged by the highest standards. In an isolated farmhouse in the Jura, Claudine awaits her husband Renaud's return from a Swiss sanatorium. She distracts herself by encouraging her young friend Annie to recount salacious episodes from her love life. When Renaud's homosexual son Marcel arrives Claudine sets about matchmaking, a fiasco she bitterly regrets.

'The realization that Colette was a major literary talent is apparent on every page.' – *Irish Times*

'*Retreat From Love* is an important book in the Colette canon, for it shows Colette becoming aware of the value of her feeling of oneness with nature and learning to express it simply and poetically.' – *Times Literary Supplement*

'With languid abandonment Colette describes sexual games played by three aristocrats . . . This English translation admirably captures the eroticism of the prose.' – *The Times*

PETER OWEN MODERN CLASSICS

GOLD
BLAISE CENDRARS
0 7206 1175 X • Paperback •128pp • £8.95

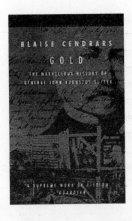

In January 1848 John Augustus Sutter, 'the first American millionaire' was ruined by one blow of a pickaxe. That blow revealed gold in one of the streams in Sutter's Californian estate, triggering the Gold Rush that brought hordes of greedy miners from every corner of the world to Sutter's vast domain.

Cendrars spent fifteen years translating Sutter's life-story into fiction, departing (often radically) from the known historical facts to reshape the story of one of the great American pioneers with the pure gold of his own imagination.

Published in 1924, *Gold* is a work of breathless pace, fantastic humour and soaring invention: an extraordinary story extraordinarily told. In 1936 Cendrars went to Hollywood to work on the movie version, *Sutter's Gold*.

'Cendrars winds the history of Europe, the Spanish Empire and the United States around his hero like a cloak of flames that throw a light on a terrifying history . . . The brevity of *Gold* is deceptive; its language is the work of a poet who can conjure up the world and its bewildering people in a paragraph.' – *New York Times Book Review*

'Cendrars' first novel remains a minor masterpiece.' – *Times Literary Supplement*

'Wise, weird and poignant . . . a wonderful modernist fable.' – *Newsweek*

URIEN'S VOYAGE
ANDRE GIDE
0 7206 1216 0 • Paperback • 94pp • £7.95

Urien's Voyage is an allegorical account of a sea voyage. From the Sargasso to the frozen Arctic, Gide charts in sensual, sumptuous prose the fantastic journey of the *Orion* and the sexual and moral transformations of those aboard. The temptations, suffering and surroundings of Urien and his companions are described with an extraordinary profusion of detail yet the pilgrims can never be sure of the reality of their experiences.

The eponymous Urien is, we now know, the young Gide himself. Written under the spell of the great French Symbolist poet Mallarmé, the novel is an illustration of both the techniques and the credo of the Symbolist movement.

'One of the most brilliant and original philosophical writers of the twentieth century.' — *New York Times*

'Sensual and erotic, even decadent.' — *Discovering World History*

'Substantial and virile . . . purity, austerity and abstraction rise to a peak.' — *The Nobel Prize Library*

'Sensuality, sexuality and pride . . . a work of art.' — *The Statesman*

'All of French thought in these past thirty years must be defined in relation to Gide.' — Jean-Paul Sartre